FROM THE NANCY DREW FILES

THE CASE: Nancy investigates a young woman's mysterious past . . . determined that the amnesia victim live to see the future.

CONTACT: Lilly Lendahl is slowly recovering her memory, but she still can't recall the identity of the person who tried to kill her.

SUSPECTS: Eric Lendahl—The family fortune is at stake, and Lilly's brother would stand to gain from his sister's death. . . .

Arch Benton—He was planning to marry Lilly, until she learned the reason he wanted her for his wife. . . .

Corie Spivey—Only one person stands in the way of her relationship with Arch Benton—Lilly Lendahl. . . .

COMPLICATIONS: Lilly may have lost her memory, but Nancy thinks some of the San Francisco police have lost their senses. They've made an arrest and shut down the investigation . . . even though Nancy knows the real culprit is still at large.

Books in the Nancy Drew Files® Series

Available from ARCHWAY Paperbacks

THE NANCY DREW FILES™

122

STRANGE MEMORIES

CAROLYN KEENE

AN ARCHWAY PAPERBACK
Published by POCKET BOOKS
New York   London   Toronto   Sydney   Tokyo   Singapore

This book is a work of fiction. Names, characters, places and incidents are products of the author's imagination or are used fictitiously. Any resemblance to actual events or locales or persons, living or dead, is entirely coincidental.

AN ARCHWAY PAPERBACK *Original*

 An Archway Paperback published by
POCKET BOOKS, a division of Simon & Schuster Inc.
1230 Avenue of the Americas, New York, NY 10020

Copyright © 1997 by Simon & Schuster Inc.
Produced by Mega-Books, Inc.

ISBN: 0-671-56880-9

First Archway Paperback printing August 1997

10 9 8 7 6 5 4 3 2 1

NANCY DREW, AN ARCHWAY PAPERBACK and colophon are registered trademarks of Simon & Schuster Inc.

THE NANCY DREW FILES is a trademark of Simon & Schuster Inc.

Cover art by Bill Schmidt

Printed in the U.S.A.

IL 6+

STRANGE
MEMORIES

Chapter

One

"I THOUGHT California was supposed to be warm!" George Fayne exclaimed, pulling her leather jacket tighter around her tall, athletic frame.

Nancy Drew laughed. "That's *southern* California," she said, correcting her friend. "San Francisco is a whole new experience in cool and damp." She was glad she had worn a white turtleneck and an oversize blue angora sweater. It was Tuesday, the girls' first day in town, and the two eighteen-year-olds were hiking through the Presidio, a wooded park near the Golden Gate Bridge. Turning toward George, Nancy gave her red-gold hair a mischievous toss. "If you didn't bring warm enough clothes for this vacation, we'll just have to hit the department stores tomorrow!"

"It's a dirty job, but somebody has to do it,"

1

George agreed, her dark brown eyes twinkling. "Besides, Bess made me promise to bring her back something." Bess Marvin was George's cousin and a close friend of Nancy.

"I'm glad Bess's family reunion wasn't on *your* side of the family," Nancy said. "It wouldn't be nearly so much fun to be in San Francisco all by myself."

"I wouldn't miss this for anything!" George exclaimed. "But you wouldn't have been alone. Your dad's here, too."

"He'll be busy with his conference," Nancy predicted. Carson Drew was a criminal attorney in River Heights, the midwestern city where the girls lived. "But it was nice of him to invite us along for the trip."

"I'll say," George replied.

"It's getting dark," Nancy said. "Maybe we should head back."

"But we'll miss watching the sun set over the water," George pointed out.

"We have ten days in San Francisco," Nancy said. "There'll be plenty of other sunsets." She stopped and craned her neck to see around some tree branches. Her backpack dropped to the ground beside her.

"What is it?" George asked. "Is something wrong?"

Nancy smiled. "Not at all," she assured George, her voice low. She gestured through a break in the pines. "Just look what a beautiful, peaceful scene that is."

George pushed aside a pine bough. Beyond the stand of trees was a rocky field starred with wildflowers. At the far end of the field, a black-haired woman sat under a tree, sketching by the last rays of the sun. She wore a flowing skirt and a loose blouse that glowed fuchsia against the green-black trees.

"She looks so intent on what she's doing," Nancy said.

"I'll bet she's talented," George said, shoving her cold fists into the pockets of her pants. "Only a real artist would freeze to death for art's sake. Come on, Nan, let's go back to the hotel, where the temperature isn't subzero."

Nancy swung her backpack onto one shoulder and headed back down the path, away from the sunset, followed by George. A few minutes later she stopped in midstride and stood perfectly still.

"What's—" George began.

Nancy cut her off with a whisper. "Listen! Someone's yelling." Her blue eyes were wide. She turned and began to retrace her steps.

"I suppose it's useless to suggest we mind our own business," George ventured.

"It might be that woman we saw before," Nancy said. "What if she needs help?" She hurried along the path with George following. Up ahead, she noticed the western sky growing dark, with only a tinge of peach remaining. Then a woman's scream pierced the twilight.

Both girls began to run. They burst through the

row of pine trees that stood between the path and the field of wildflowers. It was dark beneath the trees on the far side of the field. Nancy could make out the shape of a man standing over the woman they'd seen sketching. Something gleamed in his hand—a gun.

The man caught sight of Nancy and George racing toward him, and for a second he froze. Then he swung his gun around and slammed it against the side of the woman's head. He picked up a tote bag and took off through the trees. The woman in fuchsia slumped to the ground.

George leaped to the injured woman's side. Nancy tossed her backpack on the grass and raced into the dim woods after the man.

The man was well ahead of Nancy, tearing through the brush at a speed she knew she couldn't match. There was no path through the shadowy woods, and Nancy soon had to stop to determine in which direction the man had gone. The evening air burned cold in her lungs as she searched for signs of his passage. She spotted a bent twig and sprinted off again. After a few minutes she could hear his ragged breathing up ahead. She jumped over a fallen log; pine branches snagged her sweater and caught at her hair. Then she tripped over a root and landed facedown in the dirt.

As Nancy picked herself up, the sounds of the man's frenzied flight receded into the distance. She had lost him, and it was too dark to track him any farther in the unfamiliar landscape. She leaned against a tree and brushed the dirt off her pants as she tried to catch her breath. Then she hurried back toward George and the injured woman.

"He got away," Nancy admitted, panting, as she emerged from the trees. She looked down at the unconscious woman, who lay very still under George's leather jacket. "How is she?"

"Bad," George replied. "This head wound looks serious, and her breathing's shallow. We need to keep her warm so she won't go into shock."

"I'll run back and find a phone to call an ambulance and the police," Nancy suggested.

George shook her head. "No, let me go," she said. "You look beat. Stay with her."

Nancy nodded. As George sprinted across the field, Nancy wrapped the jacket tighter around the unconscious woman. "Don't worry," she said, though she doubted the woman could hear. "You're going to be okay."

Nancy gazed thoughtfully at the victim, wondering why she'd been attacked. The woman was about Nancy and George's age, with Asian features and translucent ivory skin. Her short, straight hair was a glossy black, except for an area above her right ear that was matted with blood.

Nancy reached into her backpack and pulled out a red bandanna, which she pressed against the woman's head wound. As she held it in place with one hand, she checked the pockets of the

5

fuchsia skirt for a clue to the wearer's identity. Unfortunately, the pockets were empty. The woman's driver's license and credit cards must have been in the tote bag the man had taken.

Her outfit was kind of offbeat, but it must have been expensive, Nancy decided. The flowing skirt and blouse were made of pure silk, Nancy saw when she checked the label of the blouse.

There might be clues in her drawings, Nancy thought, picking up the sketch pad that lay nearby.

She opened the sketchbook and slowly let out her breath. George had been right: the woman *was* a real artist. The detailed pen-and-ink drawings of San Francisco's attractions were exquisite. Nancy carefully leafed through the pages: the Golden Gate Bridge, Coit Tower, and a beautiful Victorian mansion. She flipped to the next page and stared, mesmerized. The drawing showed the prison island, Alcatraz, rising forbiddingly from San Francisco Bay. Even in the black-and-white drawing, the grim aspect of "the Rock" rolled off the page.

Unfortunately, the sketches were unsigned. Nancy guessed she wouldn't know the identity of the woman until she woke up.

An hour later Nancy and George sat in a hospital waiting room while a young police officer questioned them about what they'd seen.

"You said you chased the man through the

woods," Officer Rhonda Hayes said to Nancy. The policewoman's eyes were dark and intent in her coffee-colored face. "You must have seen more of him than your friend did."

Nancy shook her head. "I tried, but I couldn't get a good look at him," she explained. "He had dark hair, I think. He was about six feet tall, with a medium build."

The officer sighed. "The doctor says the victim will be awake in the next hour or so," she replied. "Maybe she'll give us a better description of the man who mugged her."

"This was no simple mugging," Nancy said confidently. "That woman knew the man who attacked her."

Officer Hayes shook her head. "It's unlikely that the victim was anything but a random target," she said in a reassuring voice. "We've had a string of similar incidents in and around the Presidio."

"But, Officer, we heard the man arguing with her before he hit her," Nancy said.

"The lieutenant who's handling the mugging investigation will be here soon," Hayes said. "When he comes, I'll pass on everything you've told me. But I'm sure this case will fit the pattern of those other muggings."

"But what if it wasn't random?" George asked. "That man was trying to kill her!"

"He might try again," Nancy pointed out.

"You can't let your imagination run away with

you," Officer Hayes said sympathetically. "This was just a simple mugging. Can the two of you stick around until the lieutenant arrives?"

"No problem," Nancy said. "We won't leave the hospital until we know that poor woman is going to be all right."

A few minutes after the police officer left the room, the girls looked up to see a nurse walk in.

"Dr. Kopek said a policewoman was here," the nurse began. "Is that one of you?" she asked tentatively.

Nancy and George looked at each other. Obviously the doctor meant Officer Hayes, but they couldn't pass up a chance to see the victim for themselves—and to learn more about what had happened.

George pointed to Nancy. "She's a detective," she said truthfully. Nancy had solved many cases in their hometown of River Heights.

Nancy nudged her friend. "We'd both like to see the patient," she added quickly. "Is she awake?"

"Not quite," the nurse replied as they followed her down the hall. "But she seems to be coming out of it." She led the girls into a room where the injured woman lay surrounded by tubes and instruments. The patient's eyes were closed, but she moaned softly as the nurse checked her pulse. "I'll leave you with her for a few minutes," the nurse said. "The doctor will be back shortly."

The injured woman looked even frailer than she had at the scene of the attack. Her complexion was nearly as pale as the snowy sheets, and her face was dwarfed by a thick dressing on the side of her head. Nancy sat down beside her and carefully held her hand.

Ten minutes later the door opened. The girls heard Officer Hayes's voice in the hallway outside. "Until she wakes up, or until we hear from her family or friends, this woman is a Jane Doe," she said. The officer walked into the room, followed by a gray-haired man in a white lab coat.

The doctor raised his bushy eyebrows and stared at the two girls. "And you are . . . ?" he asked.

"These are the young women who found the victim and called nine-one-one," Officer Hayes explained. She introduced the girls to Dr. Gregory Kopek. "I think they've adopted your patient," she concluded.

"Doctor, will she be all right?" Nancy asked.

"It's too early to tell," said the doctor. He turned to Officer Hayes. "She didn't lose too much blood, thanks to the efforts of her rescuers here. But her head injury is potentially serious."

"How serious?" George asked. Nancy noticed that George was nervously twisting a lock of her own short, curly hair.

"It might just be a mild concussion," said the doctor. "But there is a possibility of brain damage. I'll know more as soon as she's awake."

"She's waking up now," George said breathlessly. Everyone turned to watch as the woman's head moved weakly from side to side. Nancy lifted her hand and squeezed it gently. The patient's eyelids fluttered open. She winced and then closed them again.

"Can you hear me?" the doctor asked softly. "You've been injured. You're in the hospital, but you're going to be just fine."

"Injured?" the woman whispered, blinking rapidly. The pupils of her almond-shaped eyes were dilated.

"Somebody hurt you," said Officer Hayes.

"Hurt me?" the patient repeated, her voice barely more than a whimper.

"A man attacked you," Officer Hayes continued gently. "It's important that you tell us anything you can."

"I—I don't know," the woman said. "It's all so . . . confusing."

The officer patted her shoulder. "Take your time," she said softly.

The woman closed her eyes. "A field of wildflowers," she said softly, as if she were seeing the scene in her mind.

"What happened in that field?" asked Hayes, her pen poised to take notes.

A tear rolled down the woman's face. "I don't remember," she whispered. "Except that . . . there was a man."

"What man?" asked Hayes.

"He was . . . I don't know!" the woman cried. Her hand was trembling in Nancy's. "A man was there, but I don't remember what he looked like."

The doctor smiled reassuringly. "That's perfectly normal," he told her in a soothing voice. He turned to the others. "It's common for victims of head trauma to temporarily block out the incident in which they were injured."

"You don't understand," the woman cried. "I don't remember *anything!* I don't know who the man was." She bit her lip. Her voice dropped to a whisper. "I don't even know who *I* am!"

Chapter

Two

FIFTEEN MINUTES LATER Nancy and George were carrying cups of coffee to a table in the hospital cafeteria. They still hadn't met with the lieutenant who was investigating the case; Officer Hayes would bring him to them when he arrived.

Nancy took a long swig of coffee. She made a face. "I wonder if the coffee is this awful on purpose. It would be one way for a hospital to get customers!"

George ripped open a packet of sugar and poured it into her plastic cup. She sipped the coffee, grimaced, and tossed in the contents of two more packets. After tasting the sweetened coffee, she pushed the bowl across to Nancy. "Sugar hides the flavor," she advised.

"Too bad we can't solve that poor woman's problems so easily," Nancy said, stirring sugar into her coffee.

"What a horrible feeling it must be to have no idea who you are," George said. "What's she supposed to do while she's waiting for her memory to return?"

Nancy shrugged and shook her head. "Rest up and get her strength back, I guess," she said.

"The doctor said it could be a week or more before she remembers who she is," George said.

"True," Nancy said, "but I'll bet the police will find out her real name before that."

"How?" George asked. She smiled wryly. "By calling one of those psychic-adviser phone lines?"

Nancy laughed. "No, but her family or friends will probably file a missing-persons report soon," she said. "Then the police can match it to her description—"

Nancy stopped talking abruptly. George turned to find out what she was looking at. Officer Hayes was approaching, and close on her heels strode a tall, thin man in a wrinkled brown suit. He was looking directly at Nancy—and scowling.

"When I saw your name in Hayes's report, I hoped it was some *other* Nancy Drew," the man said in a gruff voice.

"Lieutenant Antonio!" Nancy replied with a grin. "It's good to see you again, too."

The lieutenant took the notebook from Officer Hayes. "Let me review this," he said, flipping a page. "The perpetrator had dark hair"—he stared at Nancy pointedly—"you *think*." He consulted the notebook again. "He was about six feet tall, with a *medium* build. I think I'll take the rest of the week off. This case is as good as solved."

"It was almost dark out," Nancy said with a shrug.

Antonio shook his head. "I'd have expected more details from you, Drew," he said in mock exasperation.

Nancy turned to George and Officer Hayes, who was staring. "I, uh, was involved in a case the lieutenant was investigating the last time I was in town," Nancy explained. "Lieutenant Antonio, this is my friend George Fayne."

"Pleased to meet you," George said, holding out her hand to the bushy-eyebrowed lieutenant. He gave her a curt nod. "I'm convinced Nancy has a friend in every police department in the country," George said, joking.

"Except this department," Lieutenant Antonio replied. His eyes narrowed under the thick brows. "I don't have much use for unofficial partners," he continued sternly.

"The last time Nancy was here she solved a murder, right?" George said to the lieutenant. "It sounds to me as if she was very helpful."

The lieutenant gave Nancy a long, hard stare. "She was," he admitted finally as he allowed his thin lips to curve into a grudging smile. "But remember what I said last time, Drew: I work alone. So don't get any ideas about helping out with this case."

"Lieutenant, I promise not to get into trouble," Nancy vowed. "If I find any clues to this guy's identity, I'll turn them over to you."

"You won't find any, because you won't be looking," he said.

"Okay," Nancy said. "I'll look for Jane Doe's identity instead."

The lieutenant threw up his hands. "I can't stop you, if the victim wants your help," he acknowledged. "But stay out of my way!"

"What about Jane?" George asked. "What happens to her?"

Officer Hayes shrugged. "Until someone files a missing-persons report, there's nothing the police department can do for her," she said. "She's an adult, and she's not a suspect in any crime."

"She may be released in a day or two," Nancy said, with a meaningful glance at George. "Where will she go?"

"One of the social service agencies will place her in a shelter for a few days," Officer Hayes explained.

"A shelter?" George asked. "No way! We've got a totally awesome hotel suite she can share."

"I don't think—" Antonio began.

"If the hospital releases her and she wants to stay with you, that's her prerogative," Hayes pointed out.

"Are you girls in town by yourselves?" the lieutenant asked, pursing his lips.

"No," George said carefully. "Nancy's dad is here for a conference with a bunch of other

15

lawyers." She didn't mention that Carson Drew and the other attorneys were at the Westin Saint Francis Hotel, while the girls had chosen a small, trendy inn on Washington Square.

"All right, then," the lieutenant replied. "At least a responsible adult will be around to keep an eye on you."

"As long as you're here, Lieutenant," Nancy said, "I'd like to report another crime."

He rolled his eyes. "This makes two in less than one day. Okay, what's the crime?"

"This coffee," Nancy replied, holding out her cup. "Whoever made it ought to be arrested."

Even Lieutenant Antonio laughed. "Sorry, I'm in the wrong division. You need to call Hazardous Materials."

"I didn't expect you to back down so quickly when Lieutenant Antonio said you couldn't look for the man who attacked Jane," George said to Nancy that night.

The girls were strolling along Fisherman's Wharf, looking for a place to eat a late supper. The wharf was bustling with tourists, while seagulls called raucously overhead.

"I didn't back down," Nancy pointed out. "I said I'd concentrate on figuring out who Jane is."

"And I suppose that's all you're going to concentrate on," George said, snapping a photo of a gull eating french fries off the pier.

Nancy shrugged. "If I'm looking into Jane's identity," she began, "and I happen to stumble across any other clues—well, I won't ignore them."

"But what will Attila the Cop say?" George asked.

"Antonio won't mind, as long as I don't get into trouble," Nancy replied. "That's what he's really worried about."

In her viewfinder, George framed a shot of a boy maneuvering through the crowd on a skateboard. She snapped the shutter just as he passed under a streetlamp. The photo slid into the instant camera's drying tray as they continued strolling.

"Lieutenant Antonio thinks he's supposed to act like one of those hard-boiled detective types from a Humphrey Bogart movie, but he's a good police officer. You'll like him when you get to know him," Nancy explained.

"Get to know him? Now, there's a pleasant prospect." George stopped walking abruptly. She had been gazing at the pier through the viewfinder on her camera. Now she lowered the camera and pointed at the closest restaurant. "Speaking of pleasant prospects, how about dinner?"

"On the wharf, seafood's our best bet. Especially Italian," Nancy said.

"It works for me," George agreed, and the girls resumed walking.

"There are some really good restaurants just ahead," Nancy promised. "If we can drag ourselves a few more steps."

"Until we get there, take my mind off my stomach," George urged. "Tell me your *other* plan of action—how you plan to solve the crime before Antonio does. It's too bad we have no clues."

"Wait a minute," Nancy said. "We do have one clue!" She halted abruptly, and a teenage girl with a huge radio on her shoulder nearly crashed into her. A wave of rock music poured over Nancy and George, subsiding as the girl passed.

"I forgot to turn in Jane's sketchbook," Nancy continued. She slid it out of her backpack and opened it to that afternoon's unfinished picture of wildflowers and trees. Both girls moved under a streetlamp to look at the sketch.

"Too bad she didn't sign her drawings," George said.

"Yes," Nancy agreed, flipping back a page. "But if we examine them carefully, I'm sure they can tell us something."

"There's a sketch of Fisherman's Wharf," said George.

Nancy nodded. "Jane must have been close to here when she drew this one," she replied. The sketch was of a fishing boat bobbing beside the docks, with shops and restaurants off to one side.

George focused her camera lens at the real-life scene. "I think she was sitting on one of those benches over there," George said after she had framed the scene as it was on paper.

Nancy stared at the fishing boat. "Look at that

boat, George," she said. "It's the same one that's in the sketch."

Sure enough, the weathered old boat from the drawing was docked nearby, illuminated by the lights from an open-air fish market.

George took the sketchbook from her. "It's a perfect likeness, too," she said with a nod.

"It's an *almost* perfect likeness," Nancy corrected. "But not quite. There's one crucial difference between the real boat and the one in Jane's picture."

Chapter

Three

GEORGE INSPECTED the sketch again, comparing the fishing boat on the page to the one at the dock. "Sorry, Nan," she said. "But these two boats look the same to me."

"Are you sure?" Nancy asked.

George threw up her hands. "You can't expect me to be observant when I'm weak from hunger."

"The name," Nancy said, poking a finger at the boat in the drawing. "She changed the name of the boat."

George pointed at the real boat. "It doesn't have a name—just numbers and letters."

"In Jane's sketch, that same boat has a name painted on its prow—*Lotus Flower*," Nancy said.

"You're right," George said, nodding. "And that's a much cooler name than CF-713."

Nancy scrutinized the boat in the drawing. "Originally she drew the boat with a different name on it, probably that identification number. Later she erased it and wrote the name *Lotus Flower* over it."

"What's the big deal?" George asked.

Nancy shrugged. "Nothing, I guess," she said, her expression thoughtful.

"Nan, food for thought may be enough to sustain *you* when you're hot on a case. But *I* need real food." George steered her friend toward a restaurant. "Let's eat."

The next morning Nancy called her father and told him about the strange events of the evening before.

"If anyone can help this poor woman regain her identity, it's you, Nancy," Carson Drew said after his daughter had finished telling her story. "I'll be in round-the-clock meetings for the next few days. But if you need help, don't hesitate to give me a call."

"Thanks, Dad," she replied, grateful for her father's support. After a light breakfast, Nancy and George went to the hospital to see Jane Doe.

"It's sweet of you to offer me a place to stay," Jane said to Nancy and George after they had explained their plan to her. Jane's face was pale, except for a purplish bruise that marbled her right temple, where the bandage had been before. "But it's not necessary. You don't even know me!"

21

"You're not exactly swimming in options," George pointed out. "Tomorrow, when the hospital releases you, you'll be on your own."

"And don't even think about calling an agency," Nancy said. "We've got plenty of space in our hotel suite. You're due back at the hospital for tests in a couple of days. If things aren't working out with us, you can always call the social services people later on."

"Say yes," George added. "It'll be fun! We can pretend it's a slumber party."

Jane smiled, and Nancy noticed how attractive she was. "All right," Jane agreed, "but only for a day or two."

"I'm sure we can help figure out who you are," George said.

Jane bit her lip. "Even the police can't figure it out."

"We have no choice," George told her. "Nancy is physically incapable of leaving a mystery unsolved."

"This is one mystery that may be unsolvable," Jane said, a tear glistening in one eye. "At least until I get my memory back."

"Give Nancy a chance," George said. She took a chair by the bed. "Nan, what's your plan?"

"First, let me present Exhibit Number One." Nancy reached into her backpack and, with a dramatic gesture, pulled out Jane's sketchbook. "Here, Jane. We found this beside you in the Presidio."

Jane leafed through the pages. "You mean I

drew these?" she said in disbelief. "Wow! I'm pretty good."

"You're wonderful," Nancy said, correcting her. "I'm going to use these drawings to track down your identity. And while I'm investigating, George will stay here and keep an eye on you."

Jane looked at George questioningly. "Someone might try to hurt you again," George explained. "So you shouldn't be left alone during visiting hours."

"You have no idea how frustrating this is," Jane said unhappily. "And how weird it feels to rely on people I don't know."

Nancy patted her arm. "I can imagine, but you have to trust somebody."

Jane managed a wan smile. "I do feel as if I can trust you, both of you," she admitted. "Right now you're the only friends I've got." She stretched her arms out in front of her and looked at her hands. "Just imagine, I'm an artist—and I don't even know if I can draw!"

Nancy left after making plans to meet Jane and George at the hospital at lunchtime. Then she set out to visit the sites in Jane's sketchbook. In addition to the pictures of local landmarks, the sketchbook contained drawings of less familiar places—a lovely churchyard garden, a compact white houseboat, and an interior view of a cramped, narrow room.

"It's one way of seeing the sights," Nancy said as she walked to the bus stop.

Nancy had decided not to show Jane's sketches

to Lieutenant Antonio just yet. She wanted to discover any clues hidden in the sketches, which she could then present to Antonio as solid leads.

Wisps of fog still hung in the air as Nancy hopped off the bus on Mission Street. She crossed Yerba Buena Gardens in the warm morning air and moved toward the San Francisco Museum of Modern Art.

"I'm trying to identify an assault victim who might have been at the museum recently," Nancy told a volunteer at the information desk. She held out an instant photo of Jane that George had taken that morning at the hospital. "Do you recall seeing this woman here?"

The man shook his head. "I don't remember her," he said. "But I work only a couple of days a week. Do you know when she was here?"

"No, but she drew this," Nancy said, opening the sketchbook to a meticulous copy of a painting by Henri Matisse. "I believe this painting is in your collection."

"It is," the elderly man said with a nod of recognition. "It's one of our most popular works."

"She must have spent a long time sitting in front of it, to draw such a detailed sketch," Nancy ventured. "Is there someone else who might have seen her?"

"The guard who usually works in that gallery is a friend of mine," the volunteer said. "But Jerry's out today. He's due back tomorrow."

"Thanks," Nancy said. "I'll come back then."

In the next sketch in the notebook, Nancy recognized her father's hotel, the Saint Francis. That meant the flower beds and walkways in the scene were in Union Square, which was only a few blocks away. It was a beautiful day for walking. The temperature had risen, and the early-morning fog had dissipated. The sky was a deep shade of aquamarine now.

She began showing Jane's photograph to people lounging in the square, but none of the regulars could remember seeing her there.

After leaving a message for her father at the Saint Francis, Nancy set out for Chinatown, where Jane had drawn the green-tiled dragon-topped gate on Grant Avenue, its main entrance. Again, she couldn't find anyone who recognized Jane.

Nancy gave up for the morning and took the bus back to the hospital, where she found Jane and George sharing Jane's hospital lunch.

"Hi, Nan!" George said. "Try some stewed prunes?" She held the dish out to Nancy.

Nancy collapsed in a chair and made a face. "Thanks. Some other time."

"Any luck?" asked Jane, taking a sip of chicken soup.

"I've eliminated a few dozen city residents from the list of people who might know you," Nancy replied.

"That leaves only 725,000 more to question," Jane said wryly. "You're making progress!"

"You obviously know San Francisco very

well," Nancy said, pleased that Jane had recovered enough to make jokes. "How do you feel?"

"I still have a headache, and my body is one big bruise," Jane replied. "I feel dizzy if I try to get out of bed. Other than that, I've never felt better."

"She's doing great," George said. "Whoever you are, Jane, you've got guts."

Jane shook her head sadly. "Not really," she said. "Mostly I'm just confused and disoriented."

"Well, you did manage to remember something," George said, lifting a big spoonful of Jell-O to her mouth.

"Unfortunately, it's not the least bit enlightening," Jane said. "I remember seafood. I have a strong mental image of shrimp and crabs. Bushels of them, in fact. When I think hard, I can even smell them."

Nancy's expression grew thoughtful, but she didn't say anything.

"That settles it," George said with a shrug. "Jane is a mermaid."

"Or a crab," Jane added.

"The city's full of seafood markets, but maybe . . ." Nancy's voice trailed off.

"So basically we're clueless," George said.

The telephone next to Jane's bed rang suddenly, and all three girls gave a little jump. "Who could be calling me here?" Jane asked. She picked up the handset and listened for a moment before holding it out to Nancy. "It's for you."

"Nancy Drew here." Nancy's eyes widened as she listened. "I'll be right over," she said, and put down the phone.

"What is it?" George asked.

"Lieutenant Antonio wants me to come to the police station right now."

"Testy, isn't he?" George scoffed. "I bet he's afraid you'll solve the case before he does."

"No, that's not it," Nancy said. "He's arrested a suspect in the Presidio muggings. He thinks he has the man who attacked Jane!"

Chapter

Four

TAKE YOUR TIME, Ms. Drew," said Lieutenant Antonio at the police station. He was dressed in the same rumpled brown suit he'd worn the day before.

On the other side of a one-way pane of glass, Officer Hayes led a group of five men along a wall that was marked with height indicators.

"Look at each man carefully before you make a decision," Antonio instructed Nancy.

"Number one!" Hayes called out. "Step forward."

The first man in the lineup stepped forward, turned to show his profile, and then stepped back.

"I really didn't get much of a look at the guy who hurt Jane," Nancy reminded the lieutenant.

"Number two!" Officer Hayes called.

Nancy scrutinized the men as they stepped

forward one by one. She shook her head. "I'm not sure," she said finally.

The lieutenant sighed. Then he shrugged and told Hayes to lead the men out.

"Sorry," Nancy said. "Does that mean you can't hold your suspect?"

"A victim of one of the earlier muggings picked him out of a lineup an hour ago. We can hold him for that while we collect evidence to tie him to the other crimes."

"You're still convinced that the attack on Jane is tied in to those muggings?" Nancy asked.

"'Convinced' is too strong a word," he replied. "But the attack on your new pal was carried out exactly like the other attacks, at the same time of day and in about the same location."

"That's circumstantial evidence," Nancy reminded him.

"Yes," he agreed. "But until I see hard evidence to the contrary, I assume they're linked."

"Isn't that jumping to conclusions?" Nancy asked.

"It's drawing conclusions from the evidence," Antonio said, his voice edged with irritation.

"Do you need me for anything else?" Nancy asked.

"How's Jane?" he said, not answering her question. "Is her memory beginning to return?"

Nancy shook her head. "She remembers a lot of shellfish. That's it for now."

"Beautiful," the lieutenant remarked. "I'm

trying to solve a murder case, and my star witness thinks she's Jacques Cousteau."

"She's doing the best she can," Nancy said.

"Well, you have my card," Antonio replied. "I expect you to call if she remembers anything more. And I may pay Jane Doe a visit myself in a day or two."

"Lieutenant, do you really think Jane will be safe staying with us?" Nancy asked. "If that man comes back for her—"

"As I said before, we believe we have the Presidio mugger in custody," he reminded her. "Jane will be perfectly safe."

"But what if—"

"Drew, the suspect is behind bars," the lieutenant said impatiently. "We should have enough evidence to charge him in a day or two."

"What if you don't?" Nancy asked.

"Believe it or not, the San Francisco Police Department has on occasion solved a crime on its own—without your expert assistance."

Before returning to the hospital, Nancy stopped at the sites of several other sketches in Jane's book: the Palace of Fine Arts, the Marina, and Lombard Street. Again, the photograph of Jane went unrecognized.

"I guess the chances of running into anyone who remembers me are pretty small," Jane said when Nancy got back to the hospital. "I don't exactly stand out in a crowd. Too bad I don't have green hair or a ring in my nose."

Nancy laughed. "That would make you a lot more memorable," she agreed. "But don't worry. Tomorrow I'll be talking to a guard at the art museum who might remember you."

"Do you want me to come along?" Jane asked, getting out of bed. "Maybe seeing me will jog his memory. Who knows? Maybe it'll help mine."

George shook her head. "I don't think you're ready to hike around the city," she said.

"George is right," Nancy agreed.

"You might be ready for a quick shopping trip, though," George mused. "You're going to need some clothes to wear."

"I don't have any money," Jane said in a low voice. "And I couldn't impose—"

"You can pay us back later," Nancy answered. "We won't hear any discussion about it."

"Thanks, you guys." Jane became very quiet. "This is so weird. I have no idea what kind of clothes I like."

"You were wearing a flowing silk skirt and blouse when we first saw you," Nancy said. "They were pretty. And artsy. And in lousy shape after you were attacked."

"Pink!" Jane cried suddenly. "I was wearing bright pink—like fuchsia."

"Do you remember that from when you woke up?" George asked.

"No," Jane said. "I was in a hospital gown when I woke up. I remember from the Presidio. I was wearing a hot pink skirt and blouse. They

31

were the same color as some of the flowers in the field. I remember, I really do!"

"That's great," Nancy said. "After a few more days everything will probably come back."

Jane shook her head, her brow creased. "I'm not sure I want it to, Nancy," she said slowly. She sat heavily on the bed. "I try to remember being attacked, but I can't. Only a sense of panic roars through me."

"There's no need to be scared anymore," George said. "The police told Nancy that they've caught the mugger."

"I'm not sure they've caught *my* mugger," Jane said quietly. "I have no recollection of him, but somehow I believe the police are wrong. Nancy, I think I knew the man who hit me!"

"Try to remember something about him," Nancy urged.

"I'm trying so hard," Jane said. "But he's a blank. I've just got this feeling that he wasn't a stranger."

"Take it easy, Jane," George said, placing a hand on the woman's shoulder. "Nancy's going to shake this case up."

"Shake?" Jane asked, biting her lip.

"Does that mean something to you?" asked Nancy.

"There was an earthquake," Jane said with more certainty.

"That's interesting," Nancy replied. "Do you know where you were during this earthquake?"

"No," Jane said. "I just remember a building

in ruins. I know it was an earthquake that wrecked it."

"Does that image bring anything else to mind?" Nancy asked. "Does it make you feel scared or happy?"

"That's the odd part," Jane said. "I don't feel a thing about it—not even a twinge of anxiety."

"Try this one on your memory," Nancy suggested. "Does the phrase 'lotus flower' mean anything to you?"

Jane's dark eyes grew wider. "Not exactly . . . Well, maybe it does. . . ."

"Tell me about it," Nancy urged.

"I *can't*," Jane said, her voice expressing her frustration. "I know it's the name of the boat in that sketch you showed me. But the name rings another bell in my mind, too. I just don't know why!" She slammed her right fist into her left palm.

"Don't beat yourself up about it, Jane," George said in a soothing tone. "You can't expect to remember everything all at once."

"I just wish I could remember something that made sense."

"You will," George said. "So, Nan, what's the next step?"

"I've been to nearly all the well-known attractions in Jane's sketchbook," Nancy said. "If the museum guard doesn't give me a lead tomorrow, I'll start working on the sketches that aren't instantly recognizable—houses, gardens, things like that."

"How will you know where to look?" Jane asked.

"I'll begin with the staff at our hotel," Nancy decided. "Someone might recognize one of those scenes."

"No offense, but that isn't much to go on," Jane said.

"Nancy's just getting started," George said. "Right, Nan?"

"Oh, there are plenty of things we can try," Nancy said breezily. "You're a talented artist, and you look about college age. We'll ask around at the local art schools and galleries. Maybe you're an art student."

"That's not a bad start," Jane said.

"When you're strong enough, we can take you back to the Presidio," Nancy explained. "Maybe seeing the same scenery and smelling those trees and flowers will trigger more traces of memory."

"George is right," Jane said, beginning to relax. "You really are good at this."

"And I'll bet she has a dozen more ideas," George said.

All at once Nancy did think of other options. "I saw the labels on that silk outfit you were wearing," she said. "I could try to track down the store where you bought it. Maybe a sales-clerk would—"

"What if the police are wrong and that man is still out there?" Jane asked suddenly.

"He has no way of finding you," Nancy said staunchly. "Tomorrow morning when the hospital releases you, George will pick you up and take you to our hotel. Nobody knows who we are or where we're staying. And only the police will know you're with us." She smiled reassuringly, but she didn't feel nearly so certain as she sounded.

In their hotel room that night George once again brought up the subject of Jane's attacker. "Nancy, do you really think you can find this guy?" she asked.

Nancy stood before the mirror, brushing out her long red-gold hair. Her hand slowed to a stop as she stared at her friend's reflection. "I still don't have much to go on," she admitted. "But now that the cops think they have the right man, I'm the only one who's still on this case," she said. "I don't have any choice. I have to find him."

"If robbery wasn't his motive, then what was?"

"If we knew that, we'd probably know who Jane really is," Nancy pointed out. "But I do know one thing: if he had a stronger motive than robbery for wanting to kill her, then he *will* try again."

Chapter

Five

NANCY STOOD in front of a vibrantly colored Matisse painting Thursday morning, marveling at Jane's ability to capture its essence in black and white.

"That's an excellent early example of fauvism," a voice said from behind her.

Nancy whirled around to see a uniformed security guard standing there. "Are all the guards here as knowledgeable about art as you are?" she asked.

"Some are," he said. "Can I answer any questions about the gallery for you?"

Nancy read his name tag. "You're Jerry!" she exclaimed. "You're the person I came to see."

"That's a switch," he said. "Most people come for the artwork."

"I'm trying to identify somebody," Nancy said, pulling out the photograph of Jane.

"Are you a cop?" he asked suspiciously.

"Not exactly, but I'm working with the police," Nancy replied. "Have you ever seen this woman before?" She held her breath while Jerry examined the photograph.

After a moment he nodded. "She's a pretty little thing," he said. "She was here a couple of weeks ago. She sat right over there on that bench for hours, drawing that Matisse painting."

"Who is she?" Nancy stared intently at the guard.

Jerry shrugged. "I don't know her name," he said. "We never talked about anything but art. What is this? Is she some sort of criminal? She sure didn't seem like one."

"No, she's not," Nancy assured him. "She's a witness to a crime."

"She got away without giving her name, and you're trying to track her down," he guessed.

"Something like that," Nancy replied. It would be safer for Jane if few people knew the details of her situation. "Did she ever give you a hint about who she was or where she spent her time when she wasn't here?"

"I assumed she was an art student at USF or the Art Institute or some other school," he said. "She sure is talented."

"Yes, she is," Nancy agreed.

"It's a waste, someone with that much talent working as a waitress," he said with a sigh.

"A waitress?" Nancy asked.

"I think so," he said. "She sometimes wore a kind of uniform—khaki pants and a shirt with a picture of a restaurant on it."

"What restaurant?"

He tapped his chin with his finger. "Let's see now," he said, staring at the ceiling. "The picture on the shirt was of a building. A building with a dome like the one on City Hall, only partly wrecked."

"Wrecked how?"

Jerry snapped his fingers. "I remember! It's a reproduction of a famous photo of the original City Hall, the one that was damaged in the 1906 earthquake."

"What does that have to do with a restaurant?" Nancy asked.

"It's the logo of a trendy restaurant over on Chestnut Street," Jerry said.

"Do you know the name of the restaurant?" Nancy asked.

"Sure," Jerry said. "It's the Earthquake Café."

The morning was half over, but fog still hung over the Marina District as Nancy approached the Earthquake Café. The sign in the window said Closed, but a young man in his midtwenties was standing in the open doorway, talking to somebody just inside the restaurant. He was handsome, with broad shoulders, wavy brown hair, and a confident manner.

"Excuse me. Do you work here?" Nancy asked him. "I have a couple of questions—"

"I'm sorry," he said. "I'm on my way out." He cocked his head at two people inside the restaurant. "Corie and Jack, please answer this young lady's questions," he said, his tone affable. Still, Nancy could tell he was used to having his wishes obeyed. He nodded at her, and she was taken by his hypnotic hazel eyes. For a moment her breath caught in her throat.

The man's presence had been so powerful that it was a few seconds before Nancy noticed the young man and woman now standing in the doorway—Corie and Jack, presumably. Both watched the first man move down Chestnut Street.

"Hi," Jack said, flashing Nancy a grin. He was about her age, and he was cute in an appealing boyish way, with curly black hair, sparkling green eyes, and a disarming smile.

"I'm Jack Manetti," he said. "This is Corie Spivey."

Corie was a few years older than Nancy and a few inches shorter, at about five feet four. She was blond and brown-eyed and was wearing a little too much makeup. Her close-fitting white sweater emphasized her voluptuous build.

"Sorry, but we're closed," Corie said. "We open for lunch at eleven-thirty."

"I'm not here to eat," Nancy replied before introducing herself. "I just want to ask you a few questions."

Corie motioned for Nancy to follow them inside. "Arch told us to help you, so ask away."

"Arch?" Nancy asked. "Is he the guy who just left?"

"Arch Benton," Jack supplied. "He's the owner."

"He seems kind of young to own a restaurant," Nancy remarked.

Jack smiled again. "Actually he owns six restaurants," he said. "Or his company does. He's only twenty-five, but he's president of Benton Enterprises. He inherited the firm when his father died. He's—"

"Jack, why don't you pour us some coffee?" Corie interrupted. "I swear, you're the world's worst gossip!"

Nancy stifled a laugh at Jack's exaggerated expression of remorse. Getting to know Jack Manetti might be a bonus to her investigation, she decided. "Obviously, you both work here," Nancy said.

"I'm the business manager," Corie answered. She gestured toward a booth, and she and Nancy sat down. "Jack's a waiter." She narrowed her eyes at the young man as he poured the coffee, but she was having trouble hiding a smile. "He'll be an ex-waiter if he keeps sitting down to chat with the customers," Corie added.

"She's just jealous because I get the big tips," Jack explained. As he slid into the booth next to Nancy, his arm brushed hers, and she felt a delicious tingle spread through her body.

"Dinh!" Corie called to a small, thin Asian boy, who couldn't have been more than fifteen years old. "Dinh, would you start a fresh pot of coffee for us?" The boy nodded.

"So, Nancy, what can we do for you?" Corie asked.

"I'm trying to identify a woman who was mugged in the Presidio on Tuesday evening," Nancy explained. "The woman might be an employee here. Would you mind taking a look at her photo?"

She held out the snapshot and waited for their reaction. Corie stared, her carefully plucked brows knitted together.

Jack let out a whistle. "That's Lilly Lendahl!" he exclaimed.

"She's a waitress here," Corie said. "And a friend. You say she was mugged? How badly is she hurt? Can I see her?"

"Lilly is going to be fine," she said. "But she has a head injury that's still healing, and she's a little confused. She isn't allowed to have visitors for a few days."

"I guess this explains why she hasn't shown up for work," Jack said.

"Are you with the police department?" Corie asked.

"I'm working with the police on this investigation," Nancy said carefully. "Do you know if Lilly has any enemies?"

Jack gasped. "I thought you said she was mugged."

"The police do think it was a random incident," she said. "But we still have to check out every possible angle. Can you think of anyone who would want to hurt Lilly? Someone here at the café, maybe?"

"Of course not!" Jack said vehemently. "Everyone likes Lilly. She seems so nice!"

"Seems?" Nancy asked. "I thought you worked with her."

"Jack was hired only a couple weeks ago," Corie explained. "He's still getting to know the staff."

"True," he said. "But Lilly's hard to dislike. Like you, Nancy." He was obviously flirting with her, and Nancy had to admit that she didn't mind one little bit.

Smothering a smile, Nancy looked away from his emerald eyes. "Thanks," she said, fumbling in her backpack for a notepad and pen. "But what else can you tell me about Lilly?"

"Lilly is a free spirit," Jack said. "An artistic type, like me."

"Except that Lilly has talent," Corie added.

"A minor detail." Jack waved a hand in the air. "Seriously, everyone loves Lilly. She's funny, spontaneous, kind, enthusiastic—"

"Nobody would purposely hurt Lilly," Corie concluded. "I can't believe the attack on her was anything but a mugging."

"Can you get me her employment records— an address and phone number, names of emergency contacts, and so forth?"

Corie bit her lip. "Unless you're a cop, I can't

give you Lilly's personnel records without her permission. It's against the law."

"But as her friend, can't you tell me her address, at least?" Nancy asked Corie.

The young woman slowly shook her head. "I don't know where she lives exactly."

Nancy decided not to press it. She didn't want to arouse their suspicion. After all, she had said Lilly was only a little confused.

"I'd really like to help you out," Jack confided. "But I don't know where she lives either. I am very observant, though, and maybe I've noticed something that would be useful to you. We could discuss it over cappuccino."

Corie rolled her eyes. "Subtle, Jack. Very subtle."

Nancy found herself liking Jack. She couldn't look at his sexy grin without smiling back. But making a date seemed extremely awkward under these circumstances. "I'll let you know," Nancy told him, her eyes twinkling.

A few minutes later Nancy stood on the sidewalk in front of the café. She had just checked a phone book for Lilly Lendahl, but there was no listing. Now Nancy had to decide where to go next. By now George and Lilly would be at the hotel. Nancy felt guilty about not calling Lilly immediately, but she wanted to be able to give her something more than her name when she did call.

Before Nancy could decide, she was pulled

from her thoughts by the sound of someone clearing his throat. She turned, expecting to see Jack. Instead, Dinh was slipping through the open doorway.

"Miss Drew," the boy whispered in accented English. "I heard what you said inside. You need to know more." His hands were shaking.

"I'd appreciate anything you can tell me," Nancy said. "What's wrong? Are you afraid?"

"I'm not afraid," he said, but he glanced over his shoulder.

Nancy gently steered him around the corner, where nobody could see them from the restaurant. "You seem young to have a job," Nancy said carefully. "What's your full name?"

"I'm Dinh Hai," he said. "And I'm not that young. I'm seventeen—just small."

"What did you want to tell me about Lilly?"

"She does have an enemy," he said. "Corie is the one. She pretends to be Lilly's friend, but she's not." His dark eyes blazed.

"What do you mean?"

"She talks nice when Lilly's there. But when Lilly goes away, Corie says mean things about her."

"Why does Corie dislike her?" Nancy asked. As she spoke, her mind was racing. If Corie really did have a reason to dislike Lilly, then Nancy at last had a suspect. Of course, the attacker had been a man. But Corie could have hired somebody to do the job.

"I don't know why," Dinh said, shaking his head. "But I know she's not Lilly's friend."

"Why are you telling me this?" Nancy asked.

"Lilly's my friend!" Dinh said fervently. "She brings me leftover sweets. She helps me learn English. Sometimes she even shares her tips with me."

"Why do you think Corie pretends to like her if she doesn't?"

Dinh nodded knowingly. "She wants not to anger Mr. Benton. He would be mad if he knew Corie was mean to Lilly."

"Arch Benton, the owner?" Nancy exclaimed. "Why would it matter to him if his business manager liked a waitress or not? Does he even know Lilly?"

"Oh, yes," Dinh said. "He and Lilly are, as you Americans say, a hot item."

Chapter

Six

AN HOUR LATER Nancy was sitting at a computer terminal in the public library. She had called up a database of local newspaper articles and keyed in a command to search for all mentions of a Lilly Lendahl or the Lendahl family. To her amazement the screen displayed the message "Fourteen documents found."

"Fourteen?" Nancy said out loud. She really hadn't expected to find anything.

She selected the oldest article, published more than a quarter-century earlier, and studied the text:

One of the Bay Area's rising young business leaders was married Saturday in a small private ceremony. The wedding of Eric Thomas Lendahl and Ann-Mei Kao also marks a merger between Lendahl Seafood Suppliers and the prominent Hong Kong firm of the former Miss Kao's family. Mr. Lendahl has been president and CEO of his family's firm since his father's retirement last year.

Lendahl Seafood Suppliers was founded more than a hundred years ago by Eric Lendahl's great-grandfather, a Norwegian immigrant who began the business with a single fishing boat. With the acquisition of the Kao family's company, Pacific Shellfish, the Lendahl firm now becomes a major player in the West Coast seafood industry.

Nancy turned to the next article. It was a birth announcement, dated three years later. A son, Eric Thomas Jr., was born to the Lendahls. She scrolled forward until she found another birth announcement.

"'A daughter, Lilly Mei, was born to Eric and Ann-Mei Lendahl of San Francisco,'" Nancy read aloud as she hit the button to print the file. Lilly was now twenty years old; her brother, Eric, was twenty-four.

More recent articles focused on the Lendahls' business rather than their personal lives, but several things were made clear about Lilly's parents: they were conservative, they liked to keep their personal lives private, and they were extremely wealthy.

So why is Lilly working as a waitress? Nancy asked herself, pulling out a matchbook she'd picked up at the Earthquake Café.

* * *

47

"Jack?" she said after the young waiter came to the phone. "This is Nancy Drew."

She could practically hear his grin through the receiver. "Awesome!" he said. "I was hoping you were pining away for me. Does this mean you'll go out with me after dinner for a cappuccino?"

Nancy felt warm all over when she remembered his sparkling green eyes. "I'd love to," she said truthfully.

"I'll pick you up at your hotel," he responded.

"It's a date. But I have a couple questions about Lilly. Can you spare a minute now?"

"My minute is your minute," Jack said. "Especially since Corie Legree is out running an errand."

"How much did Lilly tell you about her background?" Nancy asked, reluctant to pass on any information that Lilly might want to keep secret.

"I know her family has a lot of money," Jack said. "She never told me why she was working as a waitress. I always assumed she was slumming—seeing how the other half lives. As I said this morning, Lilly's a free spirit."

"There's a whole city full of jobs out there," Nancy said. "Do you happen to know why she chose to be a waitress at the Earthquake Café?"

"Lilly once mentioned that she's known Arch Benton all her life," Jack said. "He's an old friend of her family's."

"I see," Nancy said. She phrased her next question carefully. "Jack, do you know anything about Lilly's social life? I mean, is she dating anyone in particular?"

"I wouldn't know," Jack said. "When I'm around a pretty girl, conversation about the other men in her life is strictly forbidden. My fragile ego couldn't handle it."

"I'll keep that in mind," Nancy said dryly. There was no need to tell Jack about her long-time boyfriend, Ned Nickerson, then. While Ned was away at Emerson College, they both saw other people occasionally. Usually she warned the men she dated that her heart was already taken. But she could tell that Jack didn't want a serious relationship any more than she did.

At noontime Nancy sat in a café near Lafayette Park, drinking coffee and reviewing her notes. She looked up as Lieutenant Antonio approached.

"What did you want to talk to me about?" he asked gruffly.

"It's always great to see you, too," she said.

He rolled his eyes as he sat down across from her. "I hope you're going to make this meeting worth my while," he said, the habitual scowl on his craggy face. "Your message said you had information. Do you really think you've found something we don't already know?"

"How about Jane Doe's real name and address?" Nancy asked.

The lieutenant's mouth dropped open. "How did you manage that?"

"A lot of legwork," Nancy said.

A waitress stopped by just then to take Antonio's lunch order. As soon as she was gone, the police lieutenant turned impatiently to Nancy. "So who is our mystery woman?"

"Her name is Lilly Lendahl, and—"

"Lendahl," Antonio said, leaning forward in his chair. "Isn't there a seafood company by that name? Attached to a family fortune the size of Las Vegas?"

"That's the one," Nancy said with a nod.

Nancy consulted her notes again. "Lilly's mother is Chinese. Her father, Eric Senior, is of Norwegian descent. Lilly has an older brother, Eric Junior, who works for his father and is being groomed to become CEO one day."

"Male chauvinism," Antonio said.

"Not really. Lilly was supposed to study business administration so she could help her brother run the company one day," Nancy said. "But Lilly had different ideas."

"I bet that went over well with Mom and Pop," he said.

"Her parents—and especially her brother—were horrified when she announced that she wanted to study art."

"Where did you get this stuff?" Antonio said. "I don't remember ever reading anything about the family in the local papers."

"I found a newspaper article about a high school art award Lilly won. It mentioned that she planned to go to Berkeley. So I called the university and found a secretary in the art department who likes to gossip."

"So this is all hearsay?" Antonio asked.

"I've been able to confirm most of the facts," Nancy said. "Lilly went to Berkeley, but her parents cut off her funds when she changed her major from business to art. She moved out of the family mansion and now supports herself as a waitress."

"The poor little rich girl," he said. "You have the name of the restaurant she works at?"

"The Earthquake Café," she replied.

"Arch Benton's place. He has himself a gold mine."

"You know him?"

"Right," the lieutenant said, his voice heavy with sarcasm. "I park my yacht in the slip next to his."

"But you do know *of* him," Nancy prompted.

"Benton is a local business phenomenon," he replied. "The guy must have an army of publicity agents. You can't open a newspaper or a magazine without seeing his name."

"He took over Benton Enterprises when his father died two years ago," Nancy said. "He offered Lilly a job after her parents cut her off. Apparently he's a longtime friend of the family."

"If Benton is close to the Lendahls," Antonio pointed out, "I'm surprised he'd risk upsetting Lilly's parents by giving her a job."

"I wondered about that, too," Nancy said. "I didn't have time to do much research on Benton.

But from what I've read, I'd say he's kind of a renegade. He likes to do things his own way. Unlike Lilly's father, who is very traditional."

"So they probably don't see eye to eye on much."

"Right," said Nancy, consulting her notes. "It was Arch's father, Robert Benton, who was friends with Lilly's dad."

"Where's Lilly living now?" Antonio asked. "I mean, when she's not sharing your hotel room?"

"On a houseboat in Sausalito," Nancy replied.

"That's an odd choice for an heiress," he said.

"It was a gift from her parents on her eighteenth birthday."

Antonio rolled his eyes.

"Everything will change in about a month," Nancy explained. "That's when Lilly turns twenty-one."

"What will they give her then?" he asked. "The Golden Gate Bridge?"

"Almost," Nancy replied with a grin. "On Lilly's twenty-first birthday, or when she gets married—whichever comes first—she gets control of her trust fund. Then she can study whatever she wants, and her parents can't do anything to stop her."

"I assume she gets control of the funds only if she's considered mentally competent when the time comes," the police lieutenant said, looking thoughtful.

Nancy paused with her sandwich halfway to

her mouth. "Do you think her amnesia would affect the disbursement of that money?"

"It could," he said.

"There's a lot of money in that trust fund," Nancy reasoned. "It could provide somebody with a motive for murder."

Chapter
Seven

A MOTIVE FOR MURDER?" Lieutenant Antonio asked. "Do you still believe that someone wants Lilly Lendahl dead?" His face twisted into his familiar impatient scowl.

"I haven't ruled it out," Nancy said.

"And if the motive is control of the trust fund, then you're saying it's her parents who are trying to kill her," Antonio scoffed.

"I'm not accusing the Lendahls of anything," Nancy said. "I'm just collecting information and weighing every possibility."

"Stick to doing research," the lieutenant growled, "and leave the conclusions to the professionals."

"I want to visit the Lendahls this afternoon after I talk to Lilly," Nancy said, ignoring his outburst. "They may be mad at her, but they'll want to know what's happened."

"I should be the one to talk to them," the lieutenant said. "I hate that part of police work."

"You're welcome to come with me," Nancy said. "But I think I should be there. I'd feel funny leaving Lilly with anyone I haven't met, even her own family."

"All right, you go talk to them yourself," Antonio decided. "You've spent more time with Lilly. I'll follow up with them later."

"Would you run a background check on somebody?" Nancy asked.

"I'm not sure I'm going to like this." He sighed. "Who is it you want me to look into?" Antonio finally asked.

"Arch Benton."

"Are you out of your mind?" the lieutenant exploded. "Benton is one of the most respected businessmen in town. He's a solid citizen!"

"I didn't ask you to arrest him," Nancy pointed out. "Just check into him and his business. Doesn't it seem weird to you that he's doubled the size of his father's company in only two years?" she asked.

"What does that have to do with Lilly Lendahl?"

"Maybe nothing," Nancy said.

"This girl is a nothing in his organization. She's a waitress!"

"A waitress who's dating Benton," Nancy said.

Antonio's eyebrows shot up. "Are you sure of that?"

"Not positive," she replied. "But I think my source is solid. Isn't it standard procedure to look into any love interests of an assault victim?"

"Well, yes," Lieutenant Antonio grudgingly conceded.

Before Nancy got back to the hotel, where George and Lilly were waiting, she stopped to make a telephone call.

"Corie, may I ask you one more question about Lilly Lendahl?" she said to the business manager after identifying herself. "I've heard that she was seeing Arch Benton socially. Do you know anything about that?"

"Not really," Corie said. "What does that have to do with the man who mugged her?"

"Probably nothing," Nancy said. "But I'm surprised you didn't know they were dating. I thought you said you and Lilly were close."

"We are," Corie said. "Of course I knew she was dating Arch. I just don't have the intimate details. Even if I did . . . well, frankly, I'm not sure it's any of your business."

"I'm not asking for any intimate details," Nancy said quickly. "Is Arch in the habit of dating his employees? Or is Lilly the first?"

Corie's voice sounded strained. "You'll have to ask him," she said. "I'm only his business manager."

"Can you tell me how their relationship affects Lilly's standing among her co-workers?"

"I'm not sure what you mean."

"Dating the boss can put an employee in an awkward position," Nancy explained. "Does anyone at the Earthquake Café have reason to resent her for it?"

"Of course not!" Corie said. "Everybody loves Lilly."

"Lilly Lendahl! The name means absolutely nothing to me." Lilly looked despairingly at George and Nancy. "Are you sure you've got it right?"

While the three girls were sitting in their hotel room, Nancy patiently took Lilly over her investigations of the morning. Finally Lilly was convinced that Nancy had found out who she was.

"But I don't want to see my parents just yet, if that's okay with you," Lilly said. She flopped down on one of the big double beds and put her arm over her head. "I don't know what Lilly—I mean what *I* would say to them, especially since we're supposed to be having a fight. Could you go see them for me, Nancy?" she pleaded.

Seeing Lilly's parents alone was just what Nancy wanted to do. She glanced at her watch. "I still have time to visit their house this afternoon," she replied.

"Meanwhile, Lilly and I can check out that vintage clothing store just down the block from the hotel," George suggested. "It's about time she got out of those sweat clothes I lent her. We won't have to walk far, and we can come right back."

Lilly sat up on the edge of the bed and managed a smile. "Getting rid of the sweats sounds good," she said, teasing George. "I may have lost my memory, but I haven't completely lost my sense of style."

Nancy sat in the parlor of the Lendahl mansion in the Pacific Heights district of the city. Lilly's parents were out of the country. Her brother, Eric Junior, was sitting across from Nancy in a straight-back chair.

Eric looked older than his twenty-four years. His straight dark brown hair was thinning, and his impeccably cut suit couldn't quite hide the beginnings of a paunch. He was about six feet tall, with features that were heavier and more Caucasian than his sister's. He wore thick glasses, but it was his stuffy, serious manner that made him seem middle-aged.

Eric was concerned to hear of the attack on his sister, but he relaxed when Nancy assured him that Lilly would be fine and would recover her memory in time.

"This would never have happened if she'd done what she was supposed to," Eric pointed out.

"Are you saying business majors never get mugged?" Nancy asked.

"Of course not," Eric answered with a dismissive wave of one hand. "But what can she expect, living all by herself, hanging out in the woods at the Presidio, and working as a waitress?" He spat out the last word as if it were poison.

"You don't approve of Lilly's lifestyle?" Nancy asked.

"Lifestyle?" Eric said, shaking his head. "Lifestyle is no substitute for respectability."

"Lilly pays her own way," Nancy said. "That's respectable."

"I don't expect you to understand," Eric said, not unkindly. "Lilly disgraced us all when she rejected the family."

"I thought your parents cut her off," Nancy said.

"They had no choice. She wants to be an artist. An artist! I know she's talented," Eric went on, "but drawing is a hobby, nothing more."

"Have you or your parents talked to her since she left Berkeley?" Nancy asked.

"Absolutely not!" Eric said, raising his voice. For a moment a look of desolation crossed his face. "My mother cried for a whole week when she found out Lilly had left school." He crossed his arms in front of him. "I don't understand how Lilly can do this to us. To make matters worse, Arch Benton had the gall to help her!"

"How well do you know Arch?" Nancy asked.

"I've known him all my life," Eric said. "Our families are close friends; we supplied seafood to Arch's father way back when Robert owned only one little bistro in North Beach. Robert would never stab us in the back the way his son is doing."

"I take it you don't have much use for Arch Benton," Nancy said.

"I respect him," Eric said. "He's a good businessman. . . ." His voice trailed off.

"But?" Nancy prodded.

"But he doesn't care about anything or anyone except himself," Eric concluded. "And he has a nasty temper."

"Are you aware that Arch has been dating Lilly?" Nancy asked.

Eric jumped to his feet. "What?"

"My sources tell me they're romantically involved," Nancy said. "Is that a problem?"

Eric sat down again. "I suppose it isn't," he said slowly. "It's just that I still think of Lilly as a kid."

"She's nearly twenty-one."

"I know," he replied. "But Lilly is immature. You know, naive and trusting and impulsive. She does need someone to look after her, but Benton doesn't seem like her type."

"You're right that she needs someone to look out for her, at least for now," Nancy said. "Lilly can't stay on that houseboat by herself, without any memory. When can I bring her over here?"

Eric fixed her with a steely gaze. "When she gives up this nonsense about art school and fulfills her obligation to her family," he said.

"Until then we don't want to talk to her, and we definitely don't want to see her."

"Can't you forgive her and get on with your lives?" Nancy asked.

"Not until she changes her mind about Lendahl Seafood."

Nancy rose to her feet. "This is your sister we're talking about."

"I know I sound cold," Eric said. "But I can't let Lilly hurt my parents again. She'll be twenty-one next month. She has to face up to her responsibilities."

"And if she doesn't?"

Eric's voice was a whisper. "She'll have to make do on her own."

"That will be easier in a month, when she has a trust fund to draw on," Nancy pointed out.

"No way is she going to get her hands on that trust fund," Eric said through tight lips. "I can't allow Lendahl money to be squandered on something as frivolous as art school. I won't have it!"

"Is the money more important to you than your sister is?"

"No," Eric admitted. "But apparently it's more important to her than her family is."

"Why do you think that?" Nancy asked.

"The Lendahls have built up a company by working together as a family," Eric declared. "If she takes her trust fund and runs off to finance her new lifestyle with it, she'll be thumbing her nose at five generations of family tradition."

61

"It's Lilly's trust fund," Nancy said. "If that's her choice, there's nothing you can do to stop her."

"I'll find a way to stop her." Eric's dark eyes blazed. "I'll do whatever it takes to keep that money in the family!"

After taking a bus across the Golden Gate Bridge early that evening, Nancy led George and Lilly along the docks in Sausalito. "I'm still not convinced this is a good idea, Lilly," she said. "Are you sure you're ready for this?"

A lone seagull wheeled overhead, calling out in a loud, mournful voice. Lilly watched the bird until it disappeared behind the terraced hills that rose out of the water. Then she shook her head and turned back to her friends. "To be honest, I'm not sure of anything," she admitted.

"Maybe you should give yourself time. You don't have to remember your whole life at once," George said.

"I want to remember so badly," Lilly said. "Seeing the houseboat—seeing *my* houseboat— might bring things back. I have to try."

"Here it is!" Nancy said, pointing to a boat that gleamed white in the dusk. "I recognize it from a drawing in your sketchbook."

"It's cute," Lilly said, smiling. "I like the way it bobs against the dock." George and Nancy helped Lilly onto the gently swaying deck. Suddenly Lilly clapped a hand to her mouth.

"What's wrong?" George asked.

"How stupid of me!" Lilly said. "I don't have a key."

"The police assumed your keys were in the tote bag that the attacker stole at the Presidio," Nancy said.

"I feel so dumb," Lilly said. "We've come all this way, and now we can't get inside."

George laughed. "Relax," she said. "Nancy never goes anywhere without her lock-picking equipment."

Grinning, Nancy pulled a zippered pouch from her backpack and examined the lock to determine which tool to use. To her surprise, the door was unlocked.

Nancy pushed the door open. As she groped for the light switch, George and Lilly followed her inside. The small cabin flooded with light, and all three gasped.

"It's been ransacked!" George cried.

63

Chapter

Eight

SHOCKED, the three friends looked around at the clutter in the cabin of Lilly's houseboat. "Either someone's been here before us, or I'm the world's worst housekeeper," Lilly remarked.

The cabin was a narrow corridor with a kitchenette at one end. At the other end, a narrow door stood ajar. Nancy could see a tiny bathroom beyond it. A built-in bed and dresser lined one side of the corridor; across from them were bookshelves, a built-in desk, and a worktable. But every drawer and cabinet door hung open. Papers, clothing, and personal belongings spilled out and littered the floor. Framed photographs and unframed drawings had been hung on the walls. The ones that weren't on the floor were hanging crooked.

"Did you bring your camera?" Nancy asked George. "We'd better get photos of this."

"Sure thing," George said.

"Be careful about what you touch," Nancy said. "The police will want to dust for fingerprints."

Lilly sat down on the small, rumpled bunk. "Police?" she whispered. "I can't go through that again."

Nancy rested a hand on Lilly's shoulder. "We'll wait a bit, then," she said.

"Do you remember anything about this place?" George asked Lilly.

Lilly nodded. "I know I've seen it before."

"That's a good sign," Nancy said as she scrutinized a group of photographs that hung over the desk. "Can you tell if anything is missing?"

Lilly shook her head. "It's weird. I feel as if I saw this room from a distance before."

"Like an out-of-body experience?" George asked as she snapped a photograph.

Lilly forced a smile. "Right now I can feel the boat rocking on the water," she said as she rose unsteadily to her feet. "I can smell the ocean, and I can hear halyards clanking and seagulls calling."

"Me, too," George said. "Isn't that normal?"

"That's what I mean," Lilly said. "My recollection of the boat doesn't include any of that. My memory of it is more like gazing at a picture." Suddenly she balled her hand into a fist and pounded it against her leg. "And I know exactly why!"

"Why?" George asked, mystified.

Lilly sat on the bunk again. Then she fell back

against the pillow and stared up at the ceiling. "What I've been remembering is a picture of this place in my sketchbook!"

"It must be frustrating—" George began.

"Frustrating?" Lilly exclaimed, her voice rising. "It's driving me insane! I feel so close to remembering everything, but it just won't come!" She squeezed her eyes shut, but a tear slipped out and rolled down her face.

"It will," Nancy assured her. "Give it time."

"I don't have time," Lilly cried. "The police will ask me what's been stolen, and I won't be able to tell them!"

"We won't call them tonight, if you don't want to," Nancy decided. "We'll lock the place up when we leave, and any evidence will still be here when you're ready to talk to the lieutenant."

Lilly nodded wearily. "Thanks," she whispered, her eyes closed. A few minutes later she was breathing slowly and deeply.

Nancy and George watched as she slipped into sleep. "The slightest exertion still exhausts her," Nancy confided to George as she steered her out onto the deck so they could talk without waking Lilly.

"I'm gradually getting to know what it's like to be fabulously rich," George said. "Bess would die if she could see the beautiful clothes Lilly's got on this houseboat."

"I noticed that one of the photos over the desk is of Lilly, Eric, and their parents," Nancy said.

"I thought she wasn't speaking to them," George said.

"She's not," Nancy said. "But she wouldn't keep a family photo up on her wall if she didn't love them. She must be hoping to work things out."

"I hope so," George said. "I can't understand how family members can cut each other off like that. Did you find anything else useful?"

"There was a copy of a local business magazine on the floor near the desk," Nancy said.

"A business magazine?" George asked. "That's weird bedtime reading for an artist."

"This particular issue had a cover story about Arch Benton," Nancy said, patting her backpack. "I'm taking it with me, evidence or not."

"Speaking of good-looking guys who work for Benton Enterprises, when are you going out with that gorgeous waiter you told me about?" George asked mischievously.

Nancy grinned. "Jack and I are going to squeeze in a cappuccino later tonight," she said. "Wait till you see him, George. He's got this wild, curly dark hair and green eyes. He's really funny. I bet he's working as a waiter to put himself through drama school."

She pulled out Lilly's sketchbook. "Here's Lilly's drawing of the inside of the houseboat. Before I saw the boat, I thought the picture was of a badly designed, narrow little room."

"Look at the detail in that sketch!" George said. "Talk about meticulous. If we compare the sketchbook version to the real thing, we should know if anything's been stolen."

"Unless something was taken from inside a drawer or cupboard," Nancy reminded her.

"True," George said. "But figuring it all out will take hours. Who are your chief suspects so far?" George asked as they stared out over the water.

"Eric Lendahl has a strong motive," Nancy said. "He's hurt and bitter. He thinks Lilly has turned her back on him and their family. And he wants to get his hands on her trust fund before she spends the money on art school."

"Why should he care?" George asked. "It's not as though he needs the money."

"I don't think it's greed that's motivating him," Nancy said. "It's more like family loyalty. Anyway, I spoke to Lieutenant Antonio after I talked to Eric this afternoon. I asked him to check to see if Eric's been in trouble with the law."

"What's your gut feeling?" George asked. "Do you think Eric would try to murder his sister?"

Nancy shook her head. "No," she acknowledged with a wry chuckle. "Eric is the model-citizen type—so respectable he's boring! But anything's possible."

"What about the business manager of the café?" George asked. "You said she was only pretending to be Lilly's friend."

"So far I have no motive for her," Nancy said. "But she's a possibility, too."

"And Arch Benton?" George asked.

Nancy shrugged. "I'm having trouble getting a handle on him. From what I've heard and observed, he's very ambitious and very persuasive. And he has a temper."

"Nan, I'm afraid for Lilly," George confided. "Maybe somebody wants something from her that wasn't in her tote bag."

"I think the man took the tote bag to make the attack look like a random mugging," Nancy said. "But the key to her houseboat must have been in that tote bag."

"If robbery wasn't the motive, then why would he follow up by breaking into Lilly's houseboat?" George asked.

"Maybe to find a clue to where Lilly was," Nancy suggested grimly. "If so, then I was right to suspect that he'll come after her. When he finds her, he'll try to kill her again."

She stiffened as a soft cry sounded from the cabin. Nancy and George flew inside to find Lilly sitting up on the rumpled bunk, pushing her hair out of her eyes. George perched on the edge of the bunk. "Are you all right?"

Lilly nodded. "Yes," she said. She wasn't crying, but her face was streaked with tears. "I'm sorry I was such a basket case a few minutes ago."

"You're doing as well as anyone could, under the circumstances," George said.

"Lilly, is there anything you want to take back

to the hotel?" Nancy asked. "Clothes? Books? We'll help you gather things together."

"Yes, there is something," Lilly said. She reached into a row of books that hadn't been disturbed, technical volumes on color theory and composition. She pulled one from the shelf, and Nancy's eyes widened when she saw a smaller book behind it, shoved to the back of the bookcase. "It's my diary," Lilly explained.

Nancy grinned. "How did you know it was there?"

"Why, I just—" Lilly stopped and stared at her friends. "I—I don't know!" she stammered. "I didn't even know I was keeping a diary. I reached for it without thinking."

"See?" George said. "You really are getting your memory back. You've just got to resign yourself to the fact that you don't have any control over how fast it happens."

"I plan to read this from cover to cover tomorrow," Lilly said. "Maybe it will help me remember more."

Back at the hotel George and Lilly rode the elevator up to the girls' suite while Nancy stopped at the front desk.

"You have two messages," said the short, round man at the desk. He reached into a pigeonhole and pulled out two sealed envelopes, one blue and one white.

The return address on the first envelope was a police precinct house. Obviously it was from

Lieutenant Antonio. Nancy tore it open as she walked to the elevator. The note said that neither Arch Benton nor Eric Lendahl had ever been arrested.

So much for that idea, Nancy said to herself. She pressed the button to call the elevator and then tore open the blue envelope. She assumed it was from her father.

In the envelope was a single photograph. "You should look into this," said a scrawled note on the back. Nancy turned the photograph over and gasped. It was of a man and a woman locked in a tight embrace, kissing passionately.

It was Corie Spivey and Arch Benton.

The elevator doors opened, but Nancy ignored them and raced back to the front desk. "Who delivered this blue envelope?" Nancy asked.

The man at the desk shook his head. "I don't know," he said. "I'm not the only person who works the front desk. It might have come in when someone else was here. I'll ask my staff, if you'd like."

"Please do," Nancy said. "It's important."

As soon as she walked into the suite a few minutes later, the telephone rang. "I'll get it!" Nancy called to George and Lilly, who were in the other room. "It's probably my father."

She lifted the receiver. "Hello," she said, ready to ask Carson some legal questions about trust funds.

"Is this Nancy Drew?" said a man's muffled voice. It was definitely not her father.

"Yes, I'm Nancy," she said. "Who is this?"

"This is your only warning," the man said. "Stay out of things that don't concern you."

"Why?" Nancy asked. "What are you hiding?"

"Mind your own business!" he ordered. "Or you'll wish you had. Step out of line once more, and you'll leave more than just your heart in San Francisco!"

Chapter
Nine

"ALONE AT LAST." Jack Manetti took Nancy's hand and gazed deep into her eyes. "I thought this moment would never come."

"Stop it, Jack," Nancy said, laughing. They were seated at a small marble-topped table in a coffee bar in Washington Square. Despite his humorous manner, Nancy could tell that Jack was sincerely interested in her. Her hand felt warm and secure in his, and suddenly she was happy she had agreed to this late-night date.

Nancy leaned closer to the good-looking young man. "So what do you do when you're not waiting on tables?" she asked him.

Jack's eyes twinkled as he smiled across the table at her. "I'm waiting to be discovered," he answered promptly. "I'm an actor, in case you didn't guess."

"And you're trying out for the romantic lead?" she asked, kidding him.

Jack raised one shoulder high and scrunched up his face on one side. "Well, this week I'm auditioning for the part of Quasimodo in a neighborhood production of *The Hunchback of Notre Dame,*" he admitted. "Somehow I always end up in the character roles."

Nancy giggled as she tried to imagine him made up as the poor deformed bellringer. Jack looked at her meaningfully. "And how about you, Nancy Drew? You can't tell me this is the first time you've played the role of detective. You're too good at it."

"I've done some detecting before," she admitted.

"I knew we had something in common," Jack said. He gave her hand an extra squeeze and then released it. "We're both interested in people and why they act the way they do."

The waitress brought two cups of steaming hot cappuccino. Nancy poured a packet of sugar in hers and took a small, experimental sip. "Delicious, but super hot," she said, putting the cup down. She decided it was time to ask Jack about his fellow workers at the Earthquake Café. "As a fellow people-watcher, what can you tell me about the relationship between Corie Spivey and Arch Benton?"

Jack frowned. "I didn't know there was anything to tell," he said, running a hand through his curly hair. "He's the boss, she's the bossee. Come to think of it, they must know each other pretty well, though. He trusts her with an awful lot, especially considering . . ." Jack's voice trailed off, as if he had said too much.

"Especially considering what?" Nancy prodded him gently.

Jack's green eyes looked into hers and he smiled sheepishly. "Especially since Corie has a police record. She was arrested for assault and shoplifting when she was in her teens."

So Corie Spivey, not Arch Benton or Eric Lendahl, was the one with the record, thought Nancy. "How did you find that out, Jack? I thought you'd known Corey only a short time."

"Believe it or not, people confide in me. Today after you left, Corie went on and on about how the police were going to come snooping around the café now. I asked her why the police made her so nervous, and she spilled the story of her misspent youth. She's a model citizen today, of course, but she's still afraid."

Nancy could understand why Corie had opened up to Jack. He was warm and sympathetic and very easy to talk to. She decided not to show him the picture of Arch and Corie kissing, though, because he obviously couldn't keep a secret.

"Arch must have known about Corie's record," she said thoughtfully, "but he hired her anyway."

"Which means that Arch Benton must be a good guy as well as a smart businessman," Jack said.

Or that he likes to have a hold over his employees, Nancy added to herself.

Nancy was tired after her long day, so they chatted for a few more minutes and then Jack took her back to her hotel. When they reached the door, he turned to hold her in his arms. "Just one kiss to remember me by," he said softly, and pressed his lips lightly to hers. Nancy felt a warm tingle course through her body.

"I'd like to get to know you better, Nancy Drew," Jack said after they drew apart. "Too bad you live halfway across the country."

"We'll see each other again—I promise," Nancy said, feeling a bit breathless from the kiss. "I'll be here in San Francisco for one more week. And who knows"—she smiled up at him—"someday I may see your name up in lights."

"What would happen to Lilly's trust fund if she were to die before she turned twenty-one?" Nancy asked her father on the phone early Friday morning.

"It depends on how the document is drawn up," Carson Drew replied. "In most cases, the money would go to another family member."

"Like her brother?" Nancy asked, glancing in the mirror to fill in her lips with brownish red lipstick.

"Her brother would be a logical choice," Carson said. "But remember, I haven't seen the documents. Nancy, if Lilly is really in danger, I don't think she should be staying with you without police protection."

"The police don't believe anyone is after her," Nancy said, rooting through her jewelry bag for a pair of earrings. "And I can't convince them without solid evidence." She decided not to mention the threatening phone call she had received.

"You've got good instincts," her father told her. "Follow them. If at any time you sense that you're in danger, I want you to call in the cavalry."

"Don't worry, Dad," Nancy said. "I won't take unnecessary chances."

"I threw out the name Arch Benton among my colleagues at the conference, to see what local businesspeople think of him."

Nancy fastened a narrow gold chain around her neck and draped it over the collar of her terra-cotta wool sweater. "What did you learn?" she asked.

"They call him the Boy Wonder of Benton Enterprises."

Nancy nodded. "An article I found says that in two years he's doubled his father's holdings from three restaurants to six."

"Not only that," Carson said, "but profits at all six restaurants have gone sky-high. And there are plans to open more. People say young Mr. Benton has the magic touch."

"What do *you* say?" Nancy asked, hearing the skepticism in her father's voice.

"In my experience, magic in business consists of plain old good management . . . or foul play," he answered.

"You think Benton is crooked?" Nancy asked.

"That's more of a leap than I'm willing to make," Mr. Drew said quickly. "I hardly know anything about him. But there's usually a clear reason for such a quick, dramatic business upswing. I suggest you find that reason."

"It's weird, reading my own diary as if it were a stranger's," Lilly said at breakfast that morning. "Kind of like seeing all those sketches I can't remember drawing."

"Have you learned anything useful?" Nancy asked, spreading cream cheese on a bagel.

"I've learned that I'm a rotten journal keeper," Lilly said. "I go for days without writing at all. Then I scribble a paragraph that's so messy it looks like hieroglyphics."

"When you let me take a look at the journal, I noticed that you mentioned Arch Benton quite a few times," George said.

"I did," Lilly agreed. "I wrote that I like the way he stands up for himself, even when other people disagree with him. I don't have any recollection of this guy I'm supposedly dating. But he seems to have a lot of courage and self-confidence."

"And a temper," George reminded them.

"The magazine article called his temper 'legendary,'" Nancy said.

"I guess he never lost it with me," Lilly guessed. "But I did get angry with him."

"Why?" asked Nancy.

"I wrote that he didn't take my art seriously," Lilly said. "He thought it was a phase I'd outgrow."

Nancy rolled her eyes. "Now he sounds like Eric."

"Speaking of Arch's temper, the diary also mentioned an incident at the café," George said. "Arch yelled at a dishwasher for accidentally breaking a glass. Lilly made him stop harassing the poor kid."

"Did the diary entry give the dishwasher's name?" Nancy asked.

"Yes, but I don't remember it," George said. "It was Vietnamese, I think."

"Dinh Hai?" Nancy asked.

An awed expression lit Lilly's face. "Yes!" she cried. "I remember him!"

"From the diary?" Nancy asked.

"No, from real life!" Lilly said, trembling with excitement. "I gave him an ice-cream drink, a decadent chocolate thing called, um . . . a San Andreas Malt!"

"Dinh mentioned something like that when

I met him," Nancy said. "He's very fond of you."

"I'm fond of him, too," Lilly said. "That much I do remember."

Lilly had a full day of tests scheduled at Saint Francis Hospital. Nancy knew she'd be safe there, so she and George dropped her off and headed for Benton Enterprises.

Nancy was determined to learn more about Benton's relationship with Corie. Also, the conversation with her father had convinced her that she needed to look into Benton's business dealings. His corporate headquarters were in an office building at the Embarcadero Center, in the Financial District. Nancy and George hopped out of a taxi a block away from the building.

"Do you really think Arch Benton attacked Lilly?" George asked as they strode toward the entrance.

"I have a theory about Arch, but obviously we have no evidence against him."

"What's your theory?" George asked.

"The attack could have been a crime of passion," Nancy said. "Suppose that Lilly found out about Arch seeing Corie on the side . . ."

"She didn't write anything about that in her diary. If she suspected something, wouldn't she have written it down?" George asked.

"Maybe not. Lilly didn't write regularly. And her most recent entry was two weeks ago."

George nodded.

"Then maybe she asked Arch to meet her at the Presidio so they could talk about it," Nancy said. "They got into a fight, and Arch lost that legendary temper of his and hit her."

"It could have happened that way," George said. "But if it did, why would he ransack her houseboat?"

Nancy shook her head. "He wouldn't," she admitted.

"There's a missing piece," George said. "Something we're not seeing. But I don't know where to look for it."

"I do," Nancy said, stopping in front of the office building. "At Benton Enterprises." She lowered her voice. "I'm hoping Arch will supply that missing piece."

"You have news of Lilly Lendahl?" Arch asked eagerly after his secretary led Nancy and George into his office and introduced them. He had risen to his feet behind a sleek, modern-style desk.

Once again Nancy was struck by the presence of the man. "How much do you know about what happened?" she asked. He gestured to two chairs, and they sat down.

"A little," he said, hastily closing a folder and shoving it aside. "My employees at the Earthquake Café told me what you said to them."

"I'm sorry I didn't get a chance to meet you yesterday morning," Nancy said as she shrugged out of her jean jacket and draped it over the back of the chair.

"I'm the one who's sorry," Arch said. "Now I wish I hadn't been in such a hurry."

"You had no way of knowing Nancy had seen Lilly," George said.

The phone rang. Arch picked it up, smiled apologetically at them, and spoke for a minute. Then he cradled the phone and turned back to the girls. "How is Lilly?" he asked. "Has her memory returned?"

Nancy studied his handsome face. "I never said Lilly had amnesia, only that she was a little confused," she said. "How did you know about it?"

"I have friends on the hospital staff," he admitted.

"Did your friends tell you where Lilly's staying?" Nancy asked.

"They didn't know," Arch said. "Where is she? I want to visit her."

"I don't think that's a good idea just yet," George said. "She's still pretty confused. It might upset her."

The phone rang again, and Arch grabbed the handset. "Benton here," he said tersely. "No, I can't talk now." He hung up.

"Sorry," he said to Nancy and George. He checked his gold watch. "It's almost lunchtime. Let's run across the street for a pizza," he said. "That way, nobody can find me, and we can talk without interruptions."

As they rose to go, George nudged Nancy and

pointed to her jean jacket, which was still draped over the chair. Nancy shook her head slightly and followed Arch out the door.

Just outside the building, Nancy suddenly sighed loudly as if she'd just remembered something. "I must have left my jacket upstairs," she said, crossing her arms as if to warm herself. "You two go on to the pizza parlor. I'll join you in a minute."

George turned to Arch. "You know, Lilly remembered the oddest thing yesterday," she began quickly, hoping to distract him. She stepped off the curb. Arch glanced back at Nancy, then followed George across the street.

The secretary was on the telephone when Nancy raced in. Nancy didn't stop at her desk but went straight to Arch's door. "I forgot my jacket," she explained over her shoulder as she slipped inside Arch Benton's private office.

Nancy reached immediately for a certain folder on Arch's desk. Before he closed it, she had caught sight of a heading on a sheet of paper inside. She leafed through the contents of the folder until she saw the right one. It was a list of some sort. And at the top of the page was a heading: "Lotus Flower."

The telephone button was lighted; Arch's secretary was still taking a call. But Nancy knew that her time was limited. As soon as the secretary hung up the phone, she would burst in, wondering why Nancy was taking so long to retrieve her jacket.

Nancy ran across the room to the photocopying machine, slapped the Lotus Flower sheet and several others into the feeder on top, and punched the button to make copies. Then the light on the telephone blinked out.

Chapter

Ten

THE LAST PHOTOCOPY fell into the tray just as the button on the telephone went dark. Nancy grabbed the papers, skidded back to the desk, and shoved the originals into the folder. When the door opened, she was standing near the window, her back to Arch's secretary. Nancy had managed to pull on her jacket, and now she was slipping the copied pages inside it.

"Ms. Drew?" the secretary asked suspiciously. "Can I help you?"

Nancy spun around as if she'd been startled out of a daydream. "Oh, I'm sorry!" she said with a giggle. "I found my jacket," she said, "but then I got sidetracked by the pretty view. I didn't realize you could see the Bay Bridge from here."

The older woman scrutinized Nancy's innocent smile. "Well, I can't let you stay in here," she said finally.

"That's okay," Nancy said. "I'm supposed to meet my friend and Mr. Benton for pizza. 'Bye!"

Back across the street Nancy sat down next to George in a corner booth. "Did you order?" she asked.

"Your favorite, pepperoni," George said. "And colas all around." They paused while the waitress set their sodas on the table. "I was telling Arch about Lilly's injuries," George said casually. She shook her head imperceptibly to let Nancy know that she hadn't given him information he could use to hurt Lilly.

Arch seemed genuinely concerned. "This is terrible," he said. "Poor Lilly! I can't imagine what it would be like to lose your identity. Is there any way I can see her?"

"Not yet," George said. "But we'll tell her you asked about her."

"It seems obvious that she's staying with the two of you," Arch said. "Can you tell me where? I'd like to send flowers, to let her know I'm thinking about her."

"I don't think that would be a good idea right now," George said.

Nancy changed the subject. "I find it strange that nobody investigated when Lilly didn't show up for work on Wednesday and Thursday. Didn't you wonder where she was?"

"I'm the head of a corporation," Arch reminded her. "I don't keep track of waitresses who miss their shifts."

"Even a waitress who's your girlfriend?" Nancy asked.

"Ah, so that's it!" Arch said. "It's no secret that Lilly and I are involved."

"If you're dating, you must have noticed that she'd disappeared for two days," George said.

"Of course I noticed," Arch replied. "But you have to understand that Lilly's going through an artistic phase." He shrugged. "You know how artists are."

"No—how are they?" George asked.

"She's playing the role of rebel artist. The part includes an occasional unannounced disappearance."

Nancy took a sip of her soda. "Where does Lilly go when she disappears?"

"She doesn't vanish often," Arch said. "But now and then Lilly will suddenly run off by herself to paint in Sonoma or Carmel for a few days."

"Don't her disappearances bother you?" Nancy probed.

"Sometimes they're annoying," Arch said. "But one of the things I love best about Lilly is her spontaneity."

"I don't mean to pry," Nancy said, "but were you two having problems in your relationship?"

"No," he said firmly. "Lilly and I are very much in love. In fact, I was planning to ask her to marry me this week. It's a secret, so don't say anything to her. But I had already asked my travel agent to make reservations to Mexico for the weekend."

"That's pretty short notice," George said.

He smiled an infectious grin. "Lilly's not the only one who can be spontaneous. I wanted to whisk her away to Mexico for the weekend so that we could return on Monday as husband and wife." His face darkened. "I guess amnesia rules that out."

There was an awkward pause as the waitress returned with a large pizza. After they had helped themselves, Nancy broke the silence. "What's your relationship with Corie Spivey?" she asked.

"She's my employee," Arch answered with a shrug. "I don't have a lot of contact with her since she transferred out of the corporate office."

"When you hired Corie, did you know about her criminal record?" Nancy asked.

Arch's eyes widened. "How did you find out about that?"

"You have friends on the hospital staff," Nancy said. "I have friends in the police department." She didn't want to get Jack Manetti in trouble.

"I knew about Corie's record," Arch said. "But her honesty impressed me. So I gave her a chance."

"You didn't have any other reason for hiring her?" Nancy asked.

"What are you getting at?"

"I saw a picture of you and Corie," Nancy said, looking him in the eye. "You were kissing."

Arch took a deep breath, staring at his hands. Finally he spoke. "I hired Corie as a mailroom clerk two years ago. We dated for more than a year."

"Did Lilly know anything about that relationship?" Nancy asked.

Arch shook his head. "No. Lilly was a student at Berkeley. I hardly saw her at that time. When her folks cut her off, I gave her a job because I felt sorry for her. But suddenly I was feeling more than friendship."

Nancy nodded. "How did Corie handle your change of heart?"

"She was devastated at first," Arch said, "but she got over it. Corie and I decided not to tell Lilly we'd been a couple. We didn't want Lilly to feel responsible for our breakup."

"So Corie really likes Lilly?" Nancy asked.

"Yes, they're good friends," Arch said. "Lilly says she'd trust Corie with her life."

Nancy took a bite of her pizza and gazed thoughtfully into space. Arch's last sentence had startled her. She might have been right about a crime of passion. But what if Corie, not Arch, was behind it? Corie had lied about her relationship with Arch. And if Corie's friendship for Lilly was faked, then she certainly had a motive.

"I hear you have plans to expand your business," George said.

"I've been putting out some feelers," Arch said. "I can't complain about business. In fact, I have my eye on a little mom-and-pop place in North Beach. With an infusion of capital, that restaurant could take off."

"Do the owners want to sell?" Nancy asked.

"The owners are itching to retire," Arch said. "We'll sign the papers next week—if I can come up with the cash."

"Is that a problem?" George asked, surprised.

"Not really," Arch answered with a shrug. "I've plowed most of my assets back into the business. But I'll pull together the cash from somewhere."

"Getting married over the weekend would have made fund-raising a lot easier," Nancy said.

Arch put down his slice of pizza. "What are you driving at?"

"Lilly's trust fund," Nancy said. "She gets control of it when she turns twenty-one. Or when she gets married."

"I don't need Lilly's money!" Arch said with a scowl. He pounded his fist on the table. "I wouldn't take it if she begged me to!"

"Sorry," Nancy said. "I wasn't implying—"

"It's all right," Arch said quickly, his teeth clenched. "Lilly's trust fund is a touchy topic with me. I'm furious with her brother, Eric. He's trying to have her declared mentally incompetent, just to deprive her of her inheritance!"

"Would he do such a thing to his own sister?"

"Eric's a fanatic when it comes to family

loyalty," Arch said grimly. "He'll see her in an institution before he lets her take control of her money."

"Then Lilly's amnesia is playing right into his hands," Nancy observed.

"I'm sure it is," Arch said. "But Eric was planning this long before Lilly was attacked. He was building a case against her based on some of her flakier artistic endeavors. And he might have enough clout to institutionalize her."

"Is that one of the reasons you wanted to get married right away?"

"A quick wedding would have kept Eric from getting his hands on the money," Arch said. "But I want to marry Lilly, with or without a trust fund!"

Nancy and George watched Arch disappear into his office building. Then they turned to each other.

"Arch Benton is a total hunk!" George exclaimed with a whistle.

"Those hazel eyes take my breath away," Nancy said. "Otherwise he doesn't do a whole lot for me. He seems so cold and determined somehow."

"I know what you mean," George agreed, nodding.

"Well, thanks for helping," Nancy said. "Do you mind spending the rest of the day tracking down leads with me? Or do you have other plans?"

"Oh, you and I are going to spend the day

together," George said quickly, "but we won't be tracking down leads."

"But, George—"

"We've been working too hard. Today we're going sight-seeing, even if I have to tie you to the roof of a cable car!"

"What did you have in mind?"

"You're into criminals," George said. "Let's take the ferry across the bay to Alcatraz."

"I'll go to Alcatraz with you," Nancy said as she and George waited for the ferry at a fog-shrouded Fisherman's Wharf. "But I have one condition: I want to spend the time on the ferry working on the mystery. I need to study some papers."

"What papers?"

"I don't know yet," Nancy said. "They're photocopies of some documents that I, uh, borrowed from Arch's desk."

"Very sneaky! I guess that explains why you left your jacket in his office."

"I have another sneaky idea right now," Nancy said, catching sight of the harbormaster's office. "Will you hold my place in line? I need to check on something."

On the ferry a half hour later George was overflowing with curiosity. The girls found a quiet corner on the deck, where Nancy sat and pulled out the papers.

"'Lotus Flower,'" George read aloud, raising

her voice against the wind. "That's the name Lilly gave to the boat in her sketch. I wonder if it's really the name of a boat."

"If it is, the harbormaster's office has no record of it docking in San Francisco recently," Nancy said.

"Why is it at the top of some of these papers?" George asked, trying to shelter a page from the wind so she could read it. "What does 'Lotus Flower' have to do with Arch's business?"

"I don't know," Nancy said. "But all the items on the lists here are people's names."

"Who do you think they are?"

"I have no idea," Nancy said. She leaped to her feet and grabbed a page just before it was blown over the railing. "They could be anything—job applicants, investors, people with restaurants to sell. But I think we're going to find that these lists are not ordinary business records."

George pulled her leather jacket tight. "Is it my imagination or has the temperature dropped about six hundred degrees since we boarded this boat?"

"I've been to Alcatraz before," Nancy said. "The closer you get to the island, the worse the wind and fog seem to get."

"It's starting to rain," George said. "Let's go inside before these pages get soggy."

In the cabin they collapsed onto an empty bench, their clothes already damp. Nancy leafed through the papers. "There's a date at the top of each page," she said. "All are from the last two years."

"Do you recognize any of the names on those lists?" George asked.

"None so far," Nancy said, picking up another sheet to read. "Maybe I should ask Lieutenant Antonio to run criminal checks . . ." Her voice trailed off.

"What is it, Nan? Do you see a name you recognize?"

"Yes, I do," Nancy replied slowly, her mind racing. "It's the name of the boy who washes dishes at the Earthquake Café," she said. She looked up at her friend. "One of the people on this list is Dinh Hai."

Chapter

Eleven

THE BOAT DOCKED on Alcatraz Island before Nancy and George had time to come up with a theory about the names on Arch's list. They went ashore and walked up to the reception area of the former prison to begin the guided tour.

"This next area, Cellblock D, was known to Alcatraz prisoners as the Hole," the guide told the visitors after they'd seen the main cellblocks. He ushered a family of tourists into the first cell and shut the door behind them. Nancy and George stepped into the second cell, followed by two teenage boys. The door clanged shut.

Nancy couldn't remember being anywhere so dark. The only sounds she could hear were those of breathing—her own, George's, and that of the two high school boys. The walls and floor felt as damp and cold as if they were part of a grave.

The place even *smelled* cold. Nancy suppressed a shudder.

Normally she wouldn't have minded being stuck in a room with two good-looking guys in football letter jackets. But even the boys, who'd been talking tough just before the door clanged shut, had become subdued by the complete darkness.

"This is totally freaky," a male voice whispered. Nancy wasn't sure which boy had spoken.

She almost jumped when something brushed against her hand.

"Sorry," said the boy, who'd bumped into her. She wasn't sure it had been an accident.

"No problem," Nancy said, pulling her jacket tighter around her.

"This place is giving me a major case of the creeps," George whispered.

Suddenly a triangle of light stabbed the gloom. "Have you had enough of the Hole?" asked the cheerful voice of the park ranger.

The two boys pushed past Nancy and out of the dark cell. Then Nancy stumbled gratefully into the light, with George right behind her. As her eyes adjusted, she noticed other members of the tour group stepping from the other five cells, blinking.

"This section of Cellblock D was the ultimate in solitary confinement," the guide said in a low, theatrical voice. "Imagine being in there for as many as nineteen days straight," he continued.

"Alone in the dark. No light and no sounds, except when meals were brought in."

Nancy found herself glancing uneasily around the shadowy corridors of the decaying prison.

When the tour of the prison was over, the guide invited the visitors to spend a while exploring the island. "Take as long as you like," he said. "You have the ferry schedule. Just be sure to be at the dock at one of the times listed. If you miss the last boat of the day, you could end up spending the night here."

George shook her head. "No, thanks," she said to Nancy. "I sure wouldn't want to be stuck here after dark!"

"Me neither," Nancy agreed as they walked outside with the other visitors. "Especially in this foggy, drizzly weather. It's positively dismal!"

Nancy noticed the football players hovering a few feet away, glancing nervously at her and George. The taller of the two boys was particularly cute, with a fiery red crew cut and a sprinkling of freckles. She'd thought only cartoon action heroes had shoulders so broad. His friend, who had bright blue eyes, was sporting a tiny gold earring and a cowboy hat. Both football players seemed surprisingly shy about approaching them, probably because the girls were a year or two older.

George nudged Nancy and raised her eyebrows. "What do you think? Should we encourage Rex and Tex?" she whispered.

"Not right now, if you don't mind. I want to talk to you about Arch Benton and some other things."

"Okay," George agreed as they slipped away from the group onto a boulder-strewn path. "Maybe we can catch up with them later."

Nancy grinned.

The island was damp and rocky, with scrubby woods, low cliffs, and uninviting beaches. A map in their tour pamphlet helped them navigate their way along the trail.

"So what do you think, now that you've talked to Arch Benton himself?" George asked Nancy. "Does the Boy Wonder have a motive for attempted murder?"

"It depends on whether he's telling the truth about not needing the money in Lilly's trust fund," Nancy observed.

"He really seems to love her."

"He certainly is convincing," Nancy mused. "Of course, now that we know about him and Corie, it's clear that she has a motive, too."

"The jilted girlfriend gets revenge," George said.

"And then there's Eric," Nancy said.

"Mr. Brotherly Love Lendahl," George replied, twisting her mouth in disgust. "He wants to control that trust fund, even if he has to have his own sister committed."

"Of the three, Eric's the only one who had something to gain by sending me that photograph of Corie and Arch," Nancy acknowledged.

"You think he's trying to distract you from focusing on him and the trust fund?" George asked.

"If he's guilty, it would make sense," Nancy said. "That would also make Eric our threatening phone caller."

"How would he have known where we were staying?" George asked.

"I don't know," Nancy said. "But any one of the three could have followed us to the hotel. I've gone from having no suspects to having too many!" Nancy said.

"You'll sort it out tomorrow," George assured her. The path narrowed as they approached a steep, rocky hill. The girls had been walking side by side. Now George took the lead. "Today let's just be tourists and have some fun," she said.

At the top of the hill, the two friends found themselves on a headland that overlooked the wind-whipped bay. They stopped for a moment, panting from the exertion. Then they moved closer to the cliff's edge and gazed out over the water. In the distance the crest of the Golden Gate Bridge glowed orange, rising from a fog bank.

"I thought wind was supposed to blow fog away," Nancy said.

"It just swirls it around, like a blender," George remarked. "At least it's stopped drizzling, for now."

"Can you imagine what it would have been like to serve a life sentence on this island?"

Nancy asked. "It's always cold here. No hot, lazy summer days. No swimming in the ocean—"

"No pizza delivery," George added.

Nancy pulled out her map. "Let's head back down this other path," she suggested. "It's not as steep."

"I wonder how Lilly's doing at the hospital," George said as they resumed their hike.

"I know I'd feel better if I could find her attacker," Nancy replied.

"Then let's go over what we've got," George suggested.

"I thought you said no working on the case today," Nancy said.

"The sooner you have some answers, the sooner Lilly will be safe. I guess you could say I changed my mind. But where do we begin."

"Pick a question—any question," Nancy prompted.

"'Lotus Flower,'" George said. "What is it? Why did Lilly include it in her drawing? And why is it written across the top of Arch's mysterious list?"

"I still think the *Lotus Flower* is a real boat," Nancy said, staring into the fog.

"Then why doesn't the harbormaster have a record of its registration?"

Nancy shrugged. "I can think of a few reasons." She ticked them off on her fingers. "One: the record was lost somehow. Two: the boat is registered somewhere else. Three: it's not registered at all."

"Why wouldn't it be?" George asked.

"Maybe because it was stolen," Nancy suggested. "Or because it's being used for illegal purposes."

"Like smuggling?" George guessed. "What if Arch is the boat's owner and he's bringing something illegal into the country? But who are the people on his lists?"

Nancy pulled some of the papers from her backpack. "The names look Asian and Latino," she noticed. "I wonder if that means anything."

"Chalk it up to demographics," George suggested. "There are a lot of Asian and Latino names in California."

Nancy shook her head as she scanned one of the pages. "No," she said. "This is more than 'a lot.' It's every name on the list. That's too much of a coincidence."

"If you were a smuggler, what names would you keep on a list?" George asked.

Nancy considered the possibilities. "A list of people who buy stolen goods?" she suggested. "A crew list for the boats?"

"But how does Lilly tie into this?" George asked. "She's too nice to be a crook."

"Everyone thinks she's rebelling against her family," Nancy said.

"But smuggling is a bit more hard-core than listening to loud music or wearing clothes your mom hates," George argued.

"The other thing that bothers me about this is

that Dinh's name is on one of those lists," Nancy said. "I don't want to think he's a criminal."

"We don't know for sure that that list of names is connected to anything illegal—except perhaps, an unregistered boat," George said.

"I know. And Dinh is an employee of Benton Enterprises. It would be normal for Arch to have Dinh's name on some sort of list," Nancy acknowledged. "But if Arch *is* involved in something illegal, then Dinh might be part of it."

"Arch is very persuasive," George reminded her. "If you were new in this country, and scared, and your boss ordered you to do something—"

"Yes, it could happen that way," Nancy acknowledged. "But I hope we end up proving that Dinh and Lilly are clean."

They emerged from a clump of stunted trees onto a rocky beach. The wind tossed their hair and pulled at their damp clothes.

"This island would be the perfect setting for a gothic romance novel," Nancy suggested. "Of course, you'd have to raze what's left of the prison and build a gloomy old mansion here instead."

"Gloom is one thing this place has plenty of," George said. She pointed to a clump of stunted pines. "Forget the romance novel. How about a horror movie? Look at the way the fog twists among those trees. Can't you imagine werewolves and vampires rising from the mist?"

George had been joking, but now her laughter caught in her throat. Two hulking shapes appeared among the pines, a darker gray against the fog. They were rapidly closing in on the girls.

Nancy and George were trapped on the beach with nowhere to run.

Chapter

Twelve

Gᴇᴏʀɢᴇ ᴀɴᴅ Nᴀɴᴄʏ ғʀᴏᴢᴇ as the two forms loomed even closer.

"Hello!" called a deep voice. The two guys in letter jackets stepped out from among the trees. "Hey, it's our cellmates from solitary confinement," said the boy with the cowboy hat, the one George had dubbed Tex.

"We thought we heard voices out here," said his tall, redheaded friend.

Nancy giggled. "And we thought we were seeing ghosts."

George introduced herself and Nancy.

"My name's Kevin," the red-haired boy replied. "My friend is Ted."

The other boy tipped his Stetson. "You can call me Tex," he said.

George and Nancy swallowed their laughter.

"He's been this way ever since I let him buy

that cowboy hat," Kevin warned. He walked toward the water. "I heard San Francisco was foggy, but *this* is radical!"

Tex nodded, following his friend to the edge of the lapping waves. Tex adjusted the brim of his hat to keep the wind off his face. "The weather at home is nothing like this."

"Where's home?" Nancy asked. "Texas?"

He shook his head apologetically. "Sacramento," he admitted.

"It's starting to rain again," George said. "I can't believe we didn't bring an umbrella."

"Come back here under the trees," Kevin suggested. "It's a little drier." He led George to the edge of the woods.

Kevin was a perfect stranger, but he seemed harmless. As long as he and George remained close by, Nancy decided there was nothing to worry about.

She remained with Tex at the water's edge. He smiled at her gratefully. But now that they were alone, he had become tongue-tied.

"How long will you be in town?" she asked in a friendly tone.

"Only through the weekend," he replied. "We're here for a football game in San Bruno tomorrow."

"So you play football," she said.

"Yeah," he replied. "Second-string quarterback."

"Are you a senior?" she asked.

Tex's face, already pink from the cold, damp

wind, turned even darker. "A junior," he admitted glumly. "I guess you're a senior."

Nancy shook her head.

He looked more hopeful. "A junior?"

"I graduated," Nancy said, amused but sympathetic.

"Oh."

This boy was cute, but he couldn't carry on a conversation with an "older" woman.

Nancy glanced at George and could tell by the too-polite expression on George's face that she was totally bored. "I guess Kevin plays football, too."

"Defensive end," Tex answered. "He's a senior—MVP last week," he said enviously. "I think Kevin really likes your friend."

"Oh?" Nancy asked mischievously. "Did he say so?" She caught George's eye, along with her silent plea for rescue.

"I probably shouldn't tell you this," Tex said, "but Kevin thinks she's totally hot." He stopped, blushing again.

Nancy decided to end his misery—and George's. She stood up and gestured to her friend. "George!" she called. George smiled gratefully. "I've been thinking about what we were talking about earlier," Nancy said. "About the boats."

George hurried to the water's edge, and Kevin followed. "What do you mean?" she asked Nancy.

Nancy pointed toward the waves. "You

know," she began slowly, "if you were out there in a small boat, you could slip into this secluded little bay completely unnoticed."

"Who would want to?" Tex asked. "There's nothing on this island for anyone but tourists."

"You could use Alcatraz and the other islands in the bay as rendezvous points, places to transfer any kind of goods from one boat to another."

"I see," George said, understanding that Nancy was speaking about the possible smugglers in their case.

"Speaking of boats, there's a ferry leaving in fifteen minutes," Tex pointed out.

George peered at her watch in the fading gray light. "We need to catch it, Nan, if we're going to pick up our friend."

"You three go ahead to the ferry landing," Nancy said.

"Don't tell me you've decided to spend the night here," George said.

"Just another hour," Nancy replied. "I'll catch the last ferry."

"What's going on?" George asked.

"I think I can get a better view of Angel Island from that outcropping up there," Nancy explained. "I want to see if I can spot a likely place for a late-night rendezvous."

"Nancy is, uh, writing a novel about smugglers in this area," George lied. "That's why she's so interested in the bay."

"Do you want someone to stay with you, Nancy?" Tex asked.

"No," Nancy said. "I can get a better sense of the, uh, atmosphere if I'm alone. George, do you mind meeting our friend by yourself?"

"No," George said, "but I don't like leaving you all alone in this place."

"I'll be on the next ferry," Nancy promised. She pulled George aside as the boys started to move off. "How do you like Kevin?" Nancy whispered.

George gritted her teeth, "The fog has a higher IQ!" she whispered back. "And if I hear one more football story on the way to the boat, you are going to owe me the most expensive dinner in Chinatown!"

"You'd better hurry," Nancy said, raising her voice. "It's a long walk back to the ferry!"

"Very long," George said, rolling her eyes at Kevin's broad back.

Nancy stood on a bluff overlooking a small gravelly beach. This part of the island was deserted; because of the weather, few visitors were taking extended tours of the grounds. Through fog as dense as smoke, Nancy caught an occasional glimpse of choppy waves and another rocky island. She tried to visualize the map of San Francisco Bay superimposed over the fog-shrouded reality.

Suddenly a boat appeared in the cove, like a ghost ship in the mist. Nancy ducked behind a twisted pine tree. The small fishing boat was so dilapidated that she wondered how it stayed afloat. There were people on its deck. A lot of people. They sat huddled in groups of three and four, unprotected from the chill air and the drizzle. Nancy tried to read the markings on the boat's prow.

It was the *Lotus Flower*.

As soon as she read its name, the boat vanished behind a curtain of fog.

Nancy rose slowly, wondering if she'd imagined the whole ghostly image. She considered moving along the beach to see if she could catch another glimpse of the boat, but first she'd have to climb down from the bluff. By the time she reached the beach, the boat would probably be long gone.

In any case, it was time to make her way back to the dock. The last ferry of the day would be leaving for the mainland soon. It would feel good, she thought, to take a hot shower. Then she would change into a warm nightgown and persuade George and Lilly to stay in the suite and order room service. She started picking her way down toward the murky beach. The fog was rolling in thicker now. She could hardly see where she was going.

Just as she reached level ground, Nancy heard a twig snap behind her. Before she could react, something slammed against the side of her head.

Nancy fell, smashing her shoulder against a rock. She struggled to stand, but a man was on top of her. A powerful hand clenched the back of her head, pushing her face into the wet sand.

Nancy tried to twist her body out from under her attacker, but she was overpowered. She knew that her best bet would be to make use of her speed and agility. She had to get free. Then she could try to disable him with a well-aimed blow.

Suddenly Nancy's head was jerked to the side and pounded against a granite outcropping. The earth swayed, and for a second everything went black.

Chapter

Thirteen

NANCY BIT her bottom lip hard, and focused all of her consciousness on that tiny point of pain. Concentrating eased her dizziness.

The man gripped the back of her head again, obviously preparing to smash her temple against the wet, rough rocks. This time Nancy was ready. As he began to push her to the right, she relaxed and offered no resistance. Throwing him off-balance, she twisted her body in the opposite direction and caught him by surprise. She drew up one knee for leverage. Then she whipped her arm around, jabbing her attacker in the ribs with an elbow.

In an instant Nancy was on her feet, facing an enemy who was a dark blur in the fog. She lashed out with a perfectly timed kick to the man's abdomen. The blur crumpled. And Nancy sprinted toward the path.

She hoped the last ferry would still be waiting when she reached the dock. If not, she would have to spend the night on the cold, forbidding island—with a man who had just tried to kill her.

"Nancy!" George cried when she stumbled into their room that night. "What happened to you?"

"I decided to be a tourist today instead of a detective," Nancy said, lowering herself onto the bed. "You said it would be fun. Remember?"

"I said to hit the tourist attractions. I didn't expect them to hit back!" George said. She jumped up to fill the ice bucket with warm water.

Lilly sat beside Nancy on the bed and gently pulled back her hair. "You have some bad bruises on your head," she said. "Are you hurt anywhere else?"

"Just my shoulder," Nancy said, rubbing it. "None of my injuries are serious."

"Maybe not," George said. "But we can't take any chances with a head injury. I'll call a cab. We need to get you to a hospital."

"Stay away from that phone," Nancy ordered. "I only have a slight headache, and the scrape on my temple isn't deep. I know I don't need stitches."

"What happened?" George asked.

"Some guy jumped me on one of those se-

112

cluded beaches on Alcatraz," Nancy explained.

"Why?" Lilly demanded.

"I don't know," Nancy said. "He wasn't in the mood for a chat."

"I can't stay here any longer," Lilly decided. "It's not fair of me to put you two at risk, especially after everything you've done for me."

"Lilly, I'm fine," Nancy insisted. "I'm just a little bruised."

"At least let me call Lieutenant Antonio and your father," George suggested. "They need to know about this."

"Not tonight!" Nancy said. "If Antonio thinks I'm in danger, he'll yank me away from this case so fast I'll have whiplash. I can't afford that now that I'm so close! Believe it or not, getting beaten up is a good sign—"

"Excuse me?" George interrupted. "Maybe your head injury is worse than we thought."

"All I mean is that the attacker wouldn't have come after me unless I was close to cracking the case. I'll call my father and the lieutenant tomorrow," Nancy promised. "Tonight I just want to sleep."

"Okay, okay," George agreed. "You do look exhausted. I guess escaping from Alcatraz takes a lot out of a person."

Nancy woke early Saturday morning and dressed quietly, taking care not to disturb

George and Lilly. She noticed that Lilly's sketch-book was open to a new drawing. Nancy was glad to see that Lilly was working; drawing would help speed her recovery.

The nearly completed sketch was exquisite. It was of a small Victorian cottage with wisteria hanging from the gingerbread eaves. A profusion of daisies bloomed around an olive tree near the door. In the background Nancy could see part of a large Victorian house with ornate turrets and bay windows.

She wondered if Lilly had created the scene from her imagination or if she'd copied it. Perhaps she'd drawn it from memory. Nancy made a mental note to ask about it later; she had to move quickly now. She wanted to be long gone before George and Lilly woke up.

Nancy slipped out of the hotel room, leaving a note for her friends. Riding down Stockton Street on a Muni bus, she leaned her forehead against the cool glass of the window and reviewed her situation. Luckily, her hair covered the worst of the bruises from the night before. She didn't want to attract attention.

She guessed her attacker had been the man who'd threatened her over the phone, the same one who'd beaten Lilly. But who was he? Nobody had known that Nancy and George were going to the island. So they must have been followed.

Nancy vowed she would be more careful. She

took two buses and a cable car in a circuitous route to the subway line. Then she rode the subway several blocks and walked the rest of the way to the Embarcadero Center. She wanted to make a more thorough search of Arch Benton's office, hoping to turn up definitive evidence.

"Thank goodness they don't work on weekends," Nancy whispered at the door, noticing that the building was dark. She glanced around to make sure she was alone. Then she pulled out her tools, disabled the alarm system, and expertly picked the lock. In just a few minutes she was in.

Nancy stood in the center of Arch's office and scanned the room. She decided to start with the desk. A high-tech answering machine was attached to the telephone. Phone messages were always a good place to start. As she reached for the Play button, something on the desk near the telephone caught her eye. A phone number was scrawled across a pad of yellow self-stick notes. Nancy froze.

It was the phone number of her hotel suite.

Nancy dialed the number. "George!" she said, her voice urgent. "I'm glad I caught you before you left for breakfast. I need to tell you something—"

"Where are you?" George exploded. "Do you know how worried we've been? How could you sneak out of here without saying where you're going?"

"That's why I'm calling," Nancy said breathlessly. "George, you have to get Lilly out of our suite! And you have to do it now!"

"Why?" George asked. "What's happened?"

"Arch Benton knows where we're staying," Nancy answered, the words tumbling from her mouth. "He has our phone number on a pad by his telephone."

"Do you think it was Arch who threatened you on the phone?"

Nancy nodded. "Possibly," she said. "But I'm more worried about the threat he poses to Lilly."

"He might not pose any threat," George pointed out. "If he's telling the truth and he's really worried about her, he might have hired someone to figure out where we're staying."

"Maybe," Nancy said. "But we can't take any chances. If Arch does want Lilly dead, he'll act soon. He knows her memory is returning. If he's the one who attacked her, he can't risk her telling anyone."

"I see what you mean," George said. "And if Arch is guilty, he knows you're closing in on him. But why wouldn't he have come after us earlier? He had to have written the number on that pad yesterday."

"He was busy following us to Alcatraz. *If* he's the one we're looking for," she added.

"And if he's not?"

"Then getting Lilly out of our suite won't make the situation any worse."

"Where should I take her?" George asked.

"Take her to the Westin Saint Francis Hotel on Union Square," Nancy instructed. "Take a cab. Go to my father's room and tell him everything. Then call Lieutenant Antonio."

"Where will you be, Nan?" George asked.

"I'll meet you in my dad's room as soon as I can," Nancy promised. "But you and Lilly must leave right now!"

"All right, Nan," George said. "We're out of here."

After she hung up the phone, Nancy took a deep breath and tried to collect her thoughts. She had to make every minute count. First she listened to the messages on the answering machine; nothing there, only routine business calls. But the state-of-the-art machine stored messages digitally, and a line connected it to Arch's computer.

"Maybe the system stores messages automatically," she mused.

Nancy flicked on the computer and was relieved to see a familiar operating system. She navigated her way into the answering-machine software and discovered a week's worth of messages. Two from Tuesday afternoon caught Nancy's attention.

"Hi, Arch," Corie Spivey's voice said. "I'm at the café. I feel weird, telling you this. But the truth is, I caught Lilly eavesdropping a few minutes ago. She was listening in on one

117

of your phone calls. I thought you'd want to know."

Nancy bit her lip. Corie's tattling might have set the violence in motion. If Lilly knew Arch was involved in something illegal, he had all the more reason to keep her quiet.

I've established a possible motive for Arch to attack Lilly, Nancy thought. Now I need to show he had the opportunity.

She clicked the mouse on the screen button for Next Message, and a familiar voice filled the room.

"Arch, it's Lilly," the phone message began. Her voice was grave and intense. "I know about your secret, and I need to talk to you before it goes any further. Meet me this evening at our usual spot in the Presidio, near the wildflowers. I'll be there at sunset."

Nancy collapsed into the desk chair. Arch *was* the man who had attacked Lilly in the Presidio on Tuesday night. But what was the terrible secret Lilly had discovered?

Nancy closed the message software and pulled up a database of personnel records for the Earthquake Café.

"Now, that's interesting," she said aloud. "No unskilled kitchen employees, like Dinh Hai, are listed here. Only serving staff and managers." A cryptic entry caught her eye. "And what's this huge monthly payment marked 'RSI'?"

Nancy grabbed the phone and dialed the number for the Earthquake Café, hoping that Jack was working. She asked for him and was relieved to hear his voice.

"Hi, Jack, this is Nancy. Can I ask you a really quick question? Thanks. Where does the restaurant hire its unskilled kitchen help? I know, I know—it's a really weird question, but I need the answer."

An hour later Nancy sat in the records department at City Hall, which was open until noon on Saturdays. She was searching for documents about a local company called Restaurant Services, Inc.

According to Jack, Benton Enterprises got its unskilled kitchen help from RSI. The service firm hired and paid them, and Benton contracted for their services. A file in Arch's computer contained a list of RSI employees, including Dinh Hai, who worked at his restaurants. Every name also appeared on the lists that Nancy had photocopied the day before.

At City Hall Nancy searched a business directory, a Chamber of Commerce database, and other business records. Finally she found what she needed: RSI's annual report. There was no photograph of the company's president, but his name was listed as Ben Archer. RSI's articles of incorporation listed the same man as president.

"Ben Archer, Arch Benton," Nancy murmured as she made a copy of the report. "How transparent can you be? He must have been feeling pretty cocky about pulling this off!"

The truth was clear. Arch Benton had set up RSI as a dummy corporation to hide his criminal activities. And Nancy knew exactly what he was hiding.

Chapter

Fourteen

NANCY ARRIVED at the Earthquake Café just before the lunch rush. The first person she saw was Jack Manetti.

"Nancy!" he called, flashing her a dazzling smile. "Do you like chocolate? Let me make you a San Andreas Malt. It's on the house."

Nancy shook her head. "It sounds great, but I don't have time. Is Corie here?"

"She's in the back room, meeting with a beer distributor," Jack said.

"Do you have time to sit down and talk to me a little bit more?"

"For you, I'll make time." He led her to a booth in the back dining room. "Now, what's up?" he said as he poured coffee for both of them.

"I have some more questions about the staff," she began.

"What is this all— Wait a minute," Jack said, a concerned expression on his handsome face. He reached across the table and gently pushed back the hair at her temples. "What did you do to yourself? That's a nasty bruise!"

"I'm okay," Nancy said, reluctantly pushing his hand away. "I'll tell you about it some other time, Jack," she promised. "Right now I need to know more about the kitchen workers. Do you have any idea how long Dinh has been here?"

"Two or three months, I think," Jack said. "Why?"

"What about the rest of the unskilled kitchen staff?" she said. "Is there a lot of turnover?"

Jack nodded. "Tons," he said. "This place is extreme. We should install a revolving door in the kitchen. We had six new people start this week."

"Six people started at once?" Nancy asked. "Is that usual?"

"Somebody told me it's not unusual for Benton Enterprises. Apparently Arch hires crews of new kitchen help instead of one person at a time."

"Oh, here's Corie!" Nancy exclaimed, jumping to her feet. "I'm sorry, Jack, but I need to catch her. I'd love to see you again, but let's make a date after my investigation is wrapped up."

"I'll live for the day," he said, catching Nancy's hand in his and giving it a theatrical kiss. "Now I'm off duty, and I've got to run. I've got a *monster* audition. Yo, Spivey!" he called out. "We've got a VIP here to talk to you." He winked at Nancy and said, "That's Very Important Private Eye."

A minute later Corie had taken Jack's place at the table.

"Corie, I know you used to date Arch Benton," Nancy began after Jack had left. "Why did you lie about it to me?"

"Because you had no right to ask," Corie said, her face twisted. "I don't have to tell you anything. You're not the police."

"No, but they'll ask the same question soon," Nancy said. "It would be a lot easier if you'd talk to me. This is an investigation into an attempted murder."

"Keep the police out of this. I haven't done anything wrong!" Corie cried.

"If you haven't, then you have nothing to worry about," Nancy said. "Arch Benton is the one I'm collecting evidence against. You're his business manager. You must know what he's up to. If you help me implicate him, the police will go easy on you."

"I don't know what you're talking about," Corie protested.

"All I want is the truth," Nancy said quietly.

"The truth about what?" Corie asked, a sneer in her voice. "About the way Arch dumped me when Lilly showed up?"

"First, I want to know about Lotus Flower."

Corie froze. "What did you say?"

"Lotus Flower," Nancy said. "What does it mean?"

"I don't know," Corie said, shaking her head slowly.

"But you've heard of it," Nancy said.

"No!" Corie cried. "Well, yes. I mean"—she shrugged—"sort of."

"I need to know what it is," Nancy said. "It's important."

"I didn't think much of it at the time," Corie said slowly. "It happened early this week—Tuesday afternoon. Lilly was helping me in the back room. We overheard Arch talking on the phone in the office."

"Who was he talking to?" Nancy asked.

"I don't know," Corie said. "But it was obviously a business call. Pretty routine. Arch said he'd soon have enough kitchen help for Joplin's," Corie said. "That's his café down in the Haight."

"Did he say where he was getting the staff?" Nancy asked.

"He didn't mention it specifically," Corie said. "But we contract with a service firm for our unskilled workers. I assumed that's what he meant."

"What else do you remember?"

"Malaysia," Corie said, cocking her head. "He mentioned Malaysia."

"In what context?" Nancy asked.

"All I heard was the name of the country," she said. "His voice was muffled. And it wasn't that memorable a conversation. At least, most of it wasn't."

"But some was?"

"It was to Lilly," Corie said with a laugh. "You never know what's going to send her into one of her reveries. *Lotus Flower* did it."

"Tell me everything you remember about it."

"He said, 'The boat they'll be on is the *Lotus Flower,*'" Corie related. "I remember that part because of the effect it had on Lilly."

Nancy's heart fell to her toes. She took a deep breath. "So Lilly already knew about the *Lotus Flower,*" she said, wincing.

Corie's brow wrinkled. "No, it didn't seem that way," she said. "She just repeated the name of the boat, *Lotus Flower,* a few times, like poetry."

"I don't get it," Nancy said.

Corie shrugged. "A few minutes later she said that was a lovely name for a boat. She said she was going to draw a picture of a boat named *Lotus Flower.*"

"Was that before or after you called Arch to warn him that Lilly had been eavesdropping?"

"I never told him that," Corie protested.

"Corie, I heard your message on his answering machine," Nancy said. "I noticed you left out the part about how you were listening right along with her."

"So what?" Corie asked. "Lilly deserved it. She stole Arch from me! I wanted him to know that *I'm* the one who cares about him."

"Are you still in love with Arch Benton?" Nancy asked, feeling a grudging sympathy for the troubled woman.

"He was the best thing that ever happened to me," Corie said, tears in her eyes. "Arch was rich and handsome. And he didn't care about my past. It's not fair! Nobody ever gave me anything in my life. Lilly had everything, and she threw it all away."

"She was in love with him," Nancy said.

Corie shook her head. "Lilly told me she was going to break up with Arch the night she was mugged," Corie said.

"Corie, this could be important," Nancy said, trying to calm herself. "Think very hard about what Lilly told you."

"Lilly said that she had found out that Arch was making secret plans for them to elope to Mexico."

"Lilly wasn't pleased?"

"Lilly is a spoiled brat," Corie said. "She was all upset. She said she'd been thinking about breaking up with him for weeks because their values were too different."

"So his plans for marriage caught her by surprise?" Nancy asked.

"Completely," said Corie. "She said she couldn't believe he'd be so stupid and arrogant as to make wedding plans without asking her first."

"I think I'm getting a clear picture of what happened Tuesday," Nancy said.

"Well, I'm glad one of us knows," Corie said.

"I've learned that Arch is involved in some illegal business activities," Nancy said, deciding it was time to enlist Corie as an ally. "That's what the Lotus Flower call was about."

"What illegal activities?" Corie asked. "I can't believe that Arch—"

"On Tuesday Arch got a message from you, saying that Lilly had listened in on the Lotus Flower call. So Arch must have assumed she knew all about his secret sideline."

"But she didn't know anything!" Corie said.

"Arch didn't know that," Nancy reminded her. "At the same time, Lilly had learned that Arch was planning their wedding, so she called and left him a message. She said she knew what he was doing and she needed to talk to him before it went any further. She asked him to meet her at the Presidio."

Corie's hand flew to her mouth. "Oh, no!"

"Arch must have panicked," Nancy said. "He thought his whole operation was in danger of being uncovered. At the Presidio they began to argue, but they didn't know they were arguing about two different things.

"And then he tried to kill her."

Chapter

Fifteen

I DON'T BELIEVE YOU," Corie said. "Your story only makes sense if you believe that Arch is doing something illegal. Arch Benton is one of the most respected businesspeople in the Bay Area. Do you have any idea of the kind of profits he's pulling down?"

"Did you ever wonder how he manages it?" Nancy asked.

"He manages it by being smart and aggressive."

"I won't argue with that," Nancy said. "Setting up the illegal enterprise I've discovered took a lot of brains. And guts."

"What is this illegal enterprise?" Corie asked. "I'll bet you don't have a shred of proof that it exists."

Nancy lifted her backpack from the floor and dropped it on the table between them. She unzipped the side pouch and pulled out a folder full of papers. "Until a few minutes ago I had to assume you were involved, too. Especially with your police record."

Corie winced. "You know about my record?" she asked in a small voice. "Nancy, I'm not proud of my past. But I've straightened myself out. You have to believe that!"

"I do," Nancy said. "After hearing what you've said today, I don't think you knew anything about Arch's smuggling ring."

"You think Arch is a smuggler?" Corie asked. "That sounds like something out of a bad movie."

"But it's true," Nancy said. "These papers are lists of illegal aliens that Arch smuggled into the country. He uses some as cheap labor in his restaurants. Others he contracts out to other business owners, who may or may not know they're illegal aliens."

"This is incredible," Corie said.

Nancy pushed the folder of papers in front of her. "At the top of each page is the name of the boat and the date of its arrival," she said. "Skim these lists. You'll see some names you recognize."

"*Lotus Flower,*" Corie read aloud, her voice just above a whisper.

"Remember Malaysia?" Nancy said. "Arch's dummy corporation has so-called branch offices in Malaysia, Vietnam, and Laos, as well as Guatemala and El Salvador." She pointed to one of the pages. "See any familiar names on this list?"

"Dinh Hai," Corie said. "And the date at the top is right before he started working here."

"Do you recognize any other names?" Nancy asked.

Corie read over the list and nodded, her eyes bright with tears. "Yes," she said finally. "Four other people on this list started work here with Dinh."

"Do you believe me now?"

"I don't know what to believe," Corie said. "We hire our kitchen workers through a service firm."

"Who's your contact at RSI?" Nancy asked.

"I—I don't know," she stammered. "Arch always insists on talking to RSI himself. He told me the head of the company is an old friend of his. I figured the business arrangement was an excuse to talk about football or something."

"I have more proof," Nancy said, pulling another sheaf of papers from her backpack. "An annual report, incorporation papers, and other legal documents on RSI." She held out the incorporation papers. "Notice the name of the president."

"Ben Archer?" Corie said.

"Nobody else has a record of his existence," Nancy said. "He doesn't have a home telephone number or address. He doesn't belong to any of the obvious professional societies. He doesn't exist—except as Arch Benton. Now do you believe me?"

Corie looked defeated. "I guess I have to. What happens next?"

"We'll have a stronger case to present to the police if we can get testimony from somebody with firsthand knowledge," Nancy explained.

"That would be Arch," Corie said. "Good luck getting him to testify against himself."

"I was thinking of Dinh Hai."

A few minutes later the young dishwasher was fidgeting in the seat beside Nancy.

"Dinh, I know you care about Lilly," Nancy began. "And I know you want to help her."

Dinh nodded. "I tried to help her," he said, with a wide-eyed glance at Corie.

On a hunch Nancy asked if he knew anything about a photograph that was delivered to her hotel. Dinh shook his head.

"Listen to me," Nancy said. "It wasn't Corie who hurt Lilly. You can help Lilly by telling us the truth."

"I brought you the photo," he admitted.

"What photo?" asked Corie.

"A photo of you and Arch, kissing," Nancy explained.

Corie winced. "Which gave me a very good motive for murder," she said.

"You never liked Lilly!" Dinh lashed out at her. "You pretended to be her friend, but you weren't!"

Corie shrugged. "He's got me there," she said. "You're right, Dinh. I did resent Lilly. But I would never hurt her."

"Who did hurt her?" Dinh asked Nancy.

"We think it was Arch Benton," Corie said quietly.

Nancy took a deep breath. "Dinh, before I ask you this next question, you should know we don't want to get you in trouble. Please believe me."

The dishwasher nodded uncertainly.

"Dinh, do you have a green card?" Nancy asked.

He paled. "Mr. Benton got me out of Vietnam," he explained, his accent becoming more pronounced. "He said I would work for him. He said it was all legal."

"Did you ever see the papers?" Corie asked.

Dinh shook his head. "My reading in English is not so good," he admitted. "Mr. Benton said he would take care of everything."

"Dinh, how much money does RSI pay you?" Corie asked.

The boy looked from her to Nancy. "One dollar an hour."

Corie inhaled sharply. "That's only a fraction of what our contract with RSI calls for!"

"And it's way below the minimum wage," Nancy said. "Dinh, I know this is hard, but you have to tell the police what you've told us."

Dinh jumped up from the bench. "No!" he cried. "They'll send me back."

"They won't," Nancy said. "We'll do everything we can to help you stay in this country."

"Will Mr. Benton try to hurt Lilly again?" Dinh asked.

Nancy nodded. "He's probably looking for her right now," she said. "Luckily, he won't find her." She glanced at her watch. "In fact, I should call Lilly now, to let her and George know what we've discovered."

Nancy went to the café's pay phone and dialed the Saint Francis. Soon she heard her father's voice at the other end of the line. "Hi, Dad," she said. "Thank you for helping us out today. Can you put George on the line for a minute?"

"Excuse me?" Carson asked, sounding puzzled.

"Can I speak to George?" she asked again.

"Nancy, I don't know what you're thinking," he said, "but I haven't seen George today. I've been tied up in meetings since early this morning. This is the first break I've had all day."

"George and Lilly never got there?" Nancy asked, controlling the shaking in her voice. "Did you receive any messages from them?"

"No, nothing," he said. "Nancy, what's this about? Are you and George in trouble?"

"Dad, I'll have to call you back," Nancy said. She slammed down the receiver.

Corie and Dinh looked scared. "I'm sure everything's fine," Nancy said to reassure them. "George must have taken Lilly somewhere else where she'd be safe."

She hurriedly dialed the number of her own hotel. "This is Nancy Drew," she told the man who answered the phone. "I'm a guest there."

"Hello, Ms. Drew," the clerk said. "What can I do for you?"

"Connect me with my room, please," she said. "I need to talk to my friends."

"I can connect you," he said. "But it won't do much good. Your friends aren't there. They met a young man in the lobby this morning, and they all left together."

"What did he look like?" Nancy asked, her heart pounding.

"He was handsome," he said. "In his mid-twenties, I'd say, with brown hair."

Nancy thanked him and hung up. She turned to face Corie and Dinh, her head throbbing like a bass drum in a parade.

"What is it?" Corie asked in a choked whisper.

"We're too late," Nancy announced. "Arch Benton already has Lilly and George."

Dinh covered his face with his hands.

"Corie, I have to go after them," Nancy said. "I'll need you to call Lieutenant Antonio at this number." She wrote it down. "Get him over here with as many people as possible, and tell him everything I've told you."

"Are you kidding?" Corie objected. "He won't believe me."

"Yes, he will," Nancy told her. "He knows I'm working on this case."

"Arch Benton is a heavy hitter in this city, and

I'm a nobody!" she wailed. "A nobody with a police record!"

"I'm leaving you all the documents I've collected," Nancy assured her, patting the stack of papers on the table. "That ought to convince him. Besides, you'll have Dinh's word for it."

"And where will you be?" Corie asked.

"I'm going to Arch's house to see if he's holding Lilly and George there."

As the taxi sped toward Russian Hill, Nancy pawed through her backpack for cash to pay the driver. She bit her lip when she came across her copy of RSI's annual report. She must have missed it when she handed the other papers over to Corie. Nancy absentmindedly turned to the page that listed RSI's officers. "Ben Archer" was at the top of the list, under "President." Suddenly Nancy's eye stopped on a name halfway down the page. She gasped.

Under "Treasurer" she read a familiar name: Corie Spivey.

Nancy pounded her fist against the vinyl upholstery. "How could she have fooled me?" she whispered.

"Did you say something?" the cabdriver asked. "You look a little pale. You're not going to be sick, are you?"

Nancy shook her head. "No, I'm fine," she choked out. But her mind was racing. She'd been wrong to trust Corie Spivey. She was involved in

RSI, too, maybe as deeply involved as Arch. And Nancy had just left her with the papers that proved the existence of the smuggling ring. She'd probably already phoned Arch to warn him that Nancy was on her way to rescue Lilly and George.

She felt a tingle of recognition as the taxicab pulled up in front of Arch Benton's large Queen Anne–style Victorian house. She'd seen a drawing of it just that morning. It was the large house in the background of Lilly's latest sketch.

A dark-haired man was standing in front of the house, staring thoughtfully at the door. Nancy tensed. It was Eric Lendahl. How did he know to come here? she wondered. She wished Eric would be more cautious. If Arch was holding George and Lilly inside, the sight of Eric on his front lawn might push him into taking some sort of action.

Nancy handed a bill to the cabdriver and jumped out of the car. Crouching, she ran across the yard, following a hedge that hid her from view. The she slipped behind a hawthorn tree not far from Lilly's brother.

"Eric!" she called in a hoarse whisper. "For goodness' sake, get under cover!"

Eric whirled, staring around in confusion.

"Here!" Nancy called, motioning to him.

Eric sauntered over, unaffected by her urgency. "What are you doing here?" he asked. "It's Nancy Drew, right? Why are you hiding?"

"Get back here!" she said, grabbing him by the arm. "And keep your voice down. You could be endangering Lilly—not to mention yourself."

"Are you insane?"

"It's a long story," Nancy said. "Arch kidnapped Lilly and a friend of mine. He might be holding them inside."

Eric shook his head. "There's nobody home," he said. "I just rang the doorbell a half-dozen times. But what's this ridiculous story about—"

"Why are you here?" Nancy interrupted.

"I'm looking for my sister, if you must know," he retorted. "Is that all right with you?"

"I thought you weren't going to speak to Lilly again unless she changed her mind about her future."

Eric's face softened. "I wasn't. But I couldn't stop worrying about her, after what you said the other day. So I called the houseboat, but there was no answer," he said with a shrug. "You told me she was dating Arch. So his house seemed like a logical place to look."

"You've known Arch a long time," Nancy said. "Where else could he have taken them?"

"Taken them?" Eric asked. "Do you mean to tell me you're serious about this kidnapping thing?"

Nancy took a deep breath. "It was Arch who tried to murder Lilly at the Presidio on Tuesday," she told him. "Now I think he's planning to finish the job."

"You're hallucinating," Eric scoffed. "Arch

Benton a murderer and a kidnapper? Now I've heard everything!"

"Arch has been smuggling illegal aliens into the country to use as cheap labor in his restaurants," she said quickly. "He thought Lilly was going to blow the whistle on him."

Eric reeled as if he'd been slapped. "Maybe I'm the one who's hallucinating," he said. "I can't believe I'm hearing—"

Behind the house, a woman screamed.

"That sounded like Lilly!" Eric yelled.

Chapter

Sixteen

"WE HAVE TO CALL the police," Eric insisted.

"We don't have time." Nancy sprinted from behind the tree and skirted the house. Eric followed.

As she rounded the corner of the structure, Nancy recognized the scene from Lilly's drawing. The wisteria-draped cottage was set well back from the house and surrounded by a grove of trees. Its roof was bowed; peeling shutters dangled crookedly at the single window. But the little house was set in a lovely overgrown garden. An olive tree shaded the door.

Nancy crept up to the cottage, motioning for Eric to keep quiet. She slipped behind the olive tree and leaned against its gray-green bark to peer through the window. The first floor of the converted carriage house was all one room. Strips of afternoon sunlight outlined a back door in the far wall. Despite the little house's run-down exterior, the inside seemed well maintained, with simple furnishings and cheerful accents.

Lilly and George sat on a rag rug in the center of the room, their hands tied behind them. At their backs stood Arch Benton. He was pointing a handgun at the nape of Lilly's neck.

Behind the olive tree outside, something jostled Nancy. Before she could stop him, Eric ran to the front door. He threw it open and burst into the room. "Lilly!" he shouted.

Lilly's eyes widened in recognition. Color drained from her face. "Eric!" she cried, remembering.

"Stop right where you are, big brother!" Arch said coolly, shoving the gun against the back of Lilly's head. "Or are you trying to inherit little sister's trust fund right now?"

While Arch was busy with Eric, Nancy raced around the house to the back door. Arch had a weapon, but she had an important advantage—surprise. The door was secured with a flimsy latch. She watched through the crack along the doorframe, waiting for the right moment.

Arch held the gun on Lilly, but he spoke to Eric. "On second thought, you might not be around to collect that cash," he said. "I can't let any of you leave here, of course."

Eric grabbed for Arch's hand, but Arch was taller and heavier. He swung Eric's arm around and threw him against the wall. Eric's glasses skittered across the room.

Lilly screamed as Arch raised the gun to Eric's horrified face. His finger tensed on the trigger. Outside, Nancy took a deep breath and rammed the door with her shoulder. It flew in, slamming against the wall. "Stop right there!" she yelled from the doorway.

Arch laughed as he turned his weapon on her. "So Nancy Drew has decided to join us," he said. "Thanks for stopping by. You've saved me a trip."

"I don't understand any of this!" Lilly cried, tears running down her face.

Arch aimed the gun at his former girlfriend. Eric made a move to intervene, but Arch stopped him with a glare. "You still don't remember me, Lilly?" Arch asked.

"I-I'm beginning to," Lilly replied, her lip trembling. While Arch gazed expectantly at Lilly, Nancy carefully took a small step to one side. "It's s-so hazy," Lilly continued. "I know I used to love you, Arch. And my diary says you loved me, too. Why would you do this?"

"It's your own fault," Arch told her, his face darkening with rage. Nancy inched another step closer to him. "If you hadn't been so nosy," he continued, "I wouldn't have had to hurt you."

"You still don't have to hurt her," George told him.

"You all know too much about an operation

that depends on absolute secrecy," Arch said. "There's too much at stake now. I can't let you go to the authorities."

"I don't know what operation you're talking about," Lilly sobbed. "If I knew it before, it's gone now. I don't remember any of this!"

"Think hard, Lilly," Arch said, caressing the back of her neck with his pistol. "Try to remember why you wanted to meet me at the Presidio."

Lilly shook her head desperately. "I *can't* remember," she insisted. Then suddenly she froze and stared up at him, her mouth open. "Yes, I can," she said. "You wanted to marry me!"

"Not particularly," Arch admitted. "I mean, I *planned* to marry you but not because I wanted to."

"You were never in love with her," Eric said, his face younger and softer now that his thick glasses were gone. "You were using her."

"Lilly, despite what your brother thinks, I did love you," Arch admitted. "I admired your independence. But Eric is right about the rest. The quick rush to get married was more about money than love."

"Her trust fund?" Eric said. "You scum!"

Arch laughed. "Look who's talking," he jeered, turning the gun on Eric again. "You didn't want her to have the money either."

"I wouldn't do anything dishonest to keep it from her," Eric said.

"I'm not so sure of that," George said darkly.

"Oh, Eric's as upstanding a citizen as ever," Arch said with a chuckle. "He's not a monster. I made up the part about his trying to have his sister committed to a mental hospital."

Eric sputtered and Lilly moaned. Nancy inched closer to Arch while he was watching them. She noticed George struggling to loosen the ropes at her wrists.

"As for me, I needed a quick cash infusion," Arch said. "Lilly's trust fund was one way of getting it."

"I wouldn't have married you," Lilly told him. "I was starting to realize our values were too different. But I can't believe you'd try to kill me just because I wanted to break up."

"He didn't," Nancy announced, now that she was in position. All eyes turned to her. "He tried to kill you because he thought you knew about his criminal activities."

"What criminal activities?" Lilly asked.

"Arch and Corie set up a corporation to cover a smuggling ring," Nancy explained. "They were bringing illegal aliens like Dinh into the country."

Lilly blinked. "What?"

Arch turned to Nancy. "Me and Corie?" he asked. "Corie doesn't have the business experience to work on an operation as sophisticated as RSI."

"It's no use trying to cover for her," Nancy said. "I saw her name in the annual report."

Arch laughed. "I borrowed her name because I needed a treasurer," he said. "She doesn't know anything about it. Yet."

Nancy clenched her fists in outrage. "You were setting her up," she said accusingly. "If the authorities found out, you were going to try to pin the whole thing on Corie!"

"Very good," Arch said. "Why else would I hire an employee with a criminal record?"

"I don't understand any of this!" Lilly said again.

"You'd have remembered it soon, my dear," Arch said to her, still covering Eric with the gun.

Now they could hear sirens screaming in the distance. Obviously, Nancy thought, Corie had come through.

"You'd have remembered everything, Lilly," Arch continued. "That's why I couldn't let you live."

"You're wrong," Nancy told him. "Lilly never knew anything about RSI. She didn't understand the phone call she overheard."

"Good try, Nancy," Arch said. "But it's too late to save her skin. I know what Lilly knew. She left me a message saying she'd found out about my secret."

Lilly shook her head. "I meant your secret plan to elope to Mexico."

Nancy put her hands on her hips. "That's right, Arch. If you hadn't assumed the worst, your little private enterprise could have continued indefinitely."

Arch's mouth dropped open. He was speechless. The siren shrieks swelled to fill the silence.

"It's over, Arch," Eric said. Without his glasses, he had to squint to see the gun barrel that was pointed at his chest.

Arch's face grew hard. "It's not over until the four of you are dead," he said, taking aim.

His finger moved to the trigger, and Nancy sprang. A gunshot sounded as she launched herself at him, jerking his arm toward the floor. Behind her, Lilly screamed.

Arch staggered, swearing, when Nancy tackled him and knocked him off his feet, sending the gun clattering across the floor. He slammed a fist against her sore temple, and Nancy nearly lost her grip on him. Arch was stronger than she'd realized. She wouldn't be able to hold him by herself. Eric knew it, too. Suddenly he was there, pinning Arch's shoulders to the floor.

"Tie him with this," George said, tossing them the rope that had bound her wrists. The sirens fell silent abruptly.

Nancy winced, rubbing her head wound. "It obviously wasn't you who attacked me at Alcatraz," she said to Arch. "I managed to disable him by myself."

"That's right," Arch said as Eric bound his hands. "There's nothing worth doing that you can't pay someone to do for you."

"Except hard time," said a voice from the doorway. Lieutenant Antonio strolled in, shaking his head in disbelief. "I think I'll take the rest of the day off," he said to Officer Hayes, who followed him into the room. "These kids have things under control." He was scowling, but Nancy suspected that he was trying to cover a smile. "Ms. Drew, didn't you promise me you'd stay out of trouble?" the lieutenant asked.

"I remember hearing a similar promise," said Carson Drew, entering the carriage house. He stepped aside to allow Rhonda Hayes and another police officer to pass through, with Arch Benton between them in handcuffs, eyes on the floor.

"Are you all right, honey?" Carson asked Nancy. "I traced your call after you hung up on me. Corie Spivey, the business manager at the café, told me the whole story."

"I'm fine, Dad," Nancy said. "Everyone's fine." Arch's bullet had lodged harmlessly in the hardwood floor.

As she hugged her father, Nancy noticed that Lilly and Eric were also locked in an embrace. She caught George's eye and smiled. It seemed clear that brother and sister would work out their differences.

"Did Corie show you the proof of Arch's extracurricular activities?" Nancy asked Lieutenant Antonio.

"Yes," he said. "Nice of you to let us in on it— finally."

"You wouldn't have listened to me until I had hard evidence," Nancy reminded him.

"She's right," George said, clapping Nancy on

the shoulder. "We have it on good authority, Lieutenant, that you weren't in the market for a partner."

"Hmph!" he said to George. "Ms. Drew, your evidence was on the mark. And Corie Spivey thinks she can pull together more proof from the restaurant's business records."

"What about Dinh Hai?" Nancy asked. "If he helps the authorities, will they allow him to stay in this country?"

"Corie told me all about him," Carson said. "And I think I can help. One of my colleagues at the conference is an immigration lawyer. I'm sure I can persuade her to take on the young man's case."

"What about you, Lilly?" Nancy asked. "What will you do now?"

Lilly smiled at her brother. "Eric has asked me to move back into my parents' house in Pacific Heights," she said. "I guess I will, but only until I'm completely healed."

Eric opened his mouth to protest.

"Don't argue with me, Eric," she said with a laugh. "You know I'd drive you crazy if we lived under the same roof indefinitely. Now that I've had a taste of independence, I don't want to lose it."

"You can't mean you're going back to that houseboat?" Eric sounded incredulous.

"I haven't decided yet," Lilly said. "But I know I'll go back to school to complete my degree."

Eric sighed. "We'll talk about it," he said, wrapping an arm around his sister.

"Lieutenant," Nancy began, "do you think you'll be able to locate the rest of the players in Benton's illegal operation?"

"At any moment the FBI will raid Benton's offices. And the Coast Guard is searching for the *Lotus Flower* and the other boats." Lieutenant Antonio crossed his arms in front of his chest. "Even a rising young detective like Nancy Drew needs a little backup now and then."

This time Nancy was sure he was smiling.

Nancy's next case:

Ned's fraternity is sponsoring a murder mystery weekend at the Old Pine Inn. The idea is for actors to stage a murder, and the first guest to solve it wins a prize. For Nancy and Ned, the real prize is the chance to spend some fun romantic time together. Or that's the plan. But the weekend is about to turn deadly serious. Michael Wentworth, president of Ned's fraternity, has been invited to take part in the play. His role: murder victim. But somebody's added a dash of realism to the production—and a dash of real poison to his tea. Michael survives, but for how long? Nancy knows the drama is just beginning and that murder could still get into the act . . . in *Wicked for the Weekend,* Case #123 in The Nancy Drew Files™.

1370

R·L·STINE'S
GHOSTS OF FEAR STREET®